D0055639

This book may be kept
for 7 days only
It cannot be renewed

KNIGHTS & DRAGONS

Books by Elizabeth Spencer

FIRE IN THE MORNING

THIS CROOKED WAY

THE VOICE AT THE BACK DOOR

THE LIGHT IN THE PIAZZA

KNIGHTS & DRAGONS

A NOVEL BY

Elizabeth Spencer

KNIGHTS & DRAGONS

McGraw-Hill Book Company

NEW YORK TORONTO LONDON

Library of Congress Catalog Card Number: 65-16154

FIRST EDITION

60145

CONTENTS

part

one

I

Martha Ingram had come to Rome to escape something: George Hartwell had been certain of it from the first. He was not at all surprised to learn that the something was her divorced husband. Martha seldom spoke of him, or of the ten years she had spent with him. It was as though she feared if she touched any part of it, he would rise up out of the ground and snap at her. As it was he could sometimes be heard clear across the ocean, rumbling and growling, breathing out complaining letters and worried messengers, though what had stirred him up was not clear. Perhaps he was bored, thought Hartwell, who never wanted to meet the bastard, having grown fond of Martha, in his fussy, fatherly way. He was her superior at the U.S. cultural office, and saw her almost every day, to his pleasure.

The bastard himself Hartwell had also seen in a photograph that Martha had showed him, drawing it from her purse while lunching with him in a restaurant. But why carry his picture around? Hartwell wondered. Well, they had been talking of dogs the other day, she explained, with a little apologetic shrug and smile, and there was the dachshund she had been so fond of, there on the floor. But Hartwell, staring, was arrested by the man—that huge figure, sitting in the heavy chair with some sort of tapestry behind, the gross hands placed on the armrests, the shaggy head, and big, awkwardly tilted feet. Martha's husband! It made no sense to think about, for Martha was bright and cordial, neither slow nor light-headed, and she had a sheer look that Hartwell almost couldn't stand; he guessed it was what went with being vulnerable. "He looks German," protested Hartwell. She thought he meant the dog. "Dear old Jonesie," she said. Hartwell chuckled uneasily. "No, I meant him," he said. "Oh. Oh, yes. Well, no, Gordon is American, but it's funny your saying that. He studied in Germany and his first wife was German." "What happened to her?" Martha tucked the photograph away. "She died. . . . I was Gordon's student," she added, as though this explained something.

Why did the man keep worrying her? Why did she let him do it? Hartwell did not know, but the fact was, it did go on.

But sometimes the large figure with the shaggy head left her alone and she would be fine, and then she would get a letter from a lawyer she'd never heard of, speaking of some small lacerating matter, or an envelope addressed in a black scrawl with nothing but a clipping inside on a political issue, every word like a needle stab, considering that he knew (and never agreed with) how she felt about things. And if one thought of all the papers he had gone shuffling through to find just the right degree of what he wanted! And sometimes some admirer of his would come to Rome and say he wasn't eating at all well and would she please consider. "He never ate well," she would answer. "Only large quantities of poor food." She thought of all the hours spent carefully stirring canned cream of mushroom soup. And yet—thinker, teacher, scholar, writer, financial expert, and heaven knew what else—he had been considered great and good, and these people were, she understood, his friends. She tried to be equable and kind, and give them the right things to drink—tea, or Cinzano, or scotch—and show them around the city. "But *he* never says he would be better off if I were there," she would make them admit. "He never says it to you, or me, or anyone." Then she would be unsteady for a week or two.

Nobody can change this, she decided; it will always be this way.

But she grasped George Hartwell's sympathy, and knew that when he gave her some commission outside Rome, it was really done as a favor and made her, at least, unreachable for a time.

"Do you want to go to Genoa?" he asked her. It was June.

He was sitting at his large friendly disorderly desk, in the corner office of the consulate, and he was round and cherublike, except for a tough scraggle of thin red hair. There was always a cigar stuck in the corner of his mouth. He scrambled around among manila folders. "Arriving in Genoa," he explained, "cultural exchange people, heading eventually for Rome. But in the meantime they've excuses for wanting to see Milano, Padova, Lago di Como, perhaps going on to Venice. Italian very weak, but learning. Guide with car would be great help."

"But who are they?" She always had a feeling of hope about moving toward total strangers, as if they would tell her something good and new, and she would go away with them forever. She took the files as he found them for her. "Coggins . . . what an odd name. Richard Coggins and wife Dorothy and daughter Jean."

"That's the ones. Some friend of the family's wrote Grace about them. We've got to do something a little extra for them, but it just so happens I have to go to Florence."

Martha smiled. George's wife Grace, out of an excess of niceness, was always getting them into things. She wanted everyone to be happy, she wanted things to "work out." And so it followed, since she herself was away in Sicily, that one wound up having to be helpful for a week or two to a family named Coggins. "Mr. Coggins is an expert on opera, George, no kidding. Did you know that? Look, it says so here."

"That we should be floating somebody here to lecture the Italians on opera," George Hartwell complained. "Any six waiters in any one of a hundred trattorie in Rome can go right into the sextet from *Lucia* for fifty lire each. Italian women scream arias during childbirth. What can we tell any Italian about opera?"

"I wonder," said Martha, "if they listen to us about anything."

"Martha! That's the remark we don't ever make!" But he laughed anyway, shuffling papers. "Here we are. The others make a little more sense. . . . James E. Wilbourne and wife Rita. No children. Economist . . . thesis brought out as book: *New Economic Patterns in* . . . et cetera. He won't stick with the group much, as is more interested in factories than art galleries."

"Maybe the worst of the Coggins' is their name."

"You'll go then?"

"Yes, I'll go."

"Atta girl."

But, certainly, she thought, moving through the sharp June shadows under the trees around the consulate, something will happen to change these plans—there will be a cable in the hall or someone will have come here. She entered her summer-still apartment through all the devious stairways, corridors, and cortili that led to it. "Sequestered," George Hartwell called her, as though knowing it was not the big terrace and the view alone she had considered in taking a place one needed maps and even a compass to reach. The sun and the traffic noises were all outside, beyond the windows. There was no cable, no telephone message, but—she almost laughed—a letter. She recognized the heavy black slant of the writing and slowly, the laugh fading, slit it open. To her surprise the envelope was empty. There was nothing in it at all. He had probably meant to put a clipping in; it was a natural mistake, she thought, but some sort of menace was what she felt, being permanently lodged in the mind of a person whose love had turned to rejection. "Forget it," Hartwell had advised her. "Everybody has something to forget." But, alas, she was intellectually as well as emotionally tenacious and she had, furthermore, her question to address to the sky: how can love, in the first place, turn into hate, and how can I, so trapped in hatred, not suffer for it?

In his apartment, the expensive, oak-panelled, high-ceilinged place in New York's upper Seventies, crusted with books and littered with ash trays, she had lived out a life of corners, and tiny chores had lengthened before her like shadows drawn out into a sunslant; she had worn sweaters that shrank in the back and coloured blouses that faded or white ones that turned grey, had entertained noble feelings toward all his friends, and tried to get in step with the ponderous designs he put life to, like training hippopotami to jump through hoops. There had been the long rainy afternoons, the kindness of the porter, the illness of the dog, the thin slashing of the brass elevator doors, the walks in the park. She still felt small in doorways. Not wanting to spend a lot, he had had her watched by a cut-rate detective agency, whose agent she had not only discovered at it, but made friends with.

She crumpled the empty envelope and dropped it in the wastebasket, bringing herself up with a determined shake rather like a shudder.

2

Martha *Ingram* would always remember the first sight she had of her new Americans at the dock in Genoa. She got a chance to look them over before they saw her. She had to smile—it was so obviously "them." They stood together in clothes that had seen too much of the insides of suitcases and small metal closets in ship cabins; they were pale from getting up early after an almost sleepless night at sea, and the early breakfast after the boat had gone still, the worry over the luggage, would have made them almost sick. The voyage was already a memory; they waved halfheartedly, in a puzzled way, to a couple who, for ten days, must have seemed their most intimate friends. They formed their little huddle, their baggage piling slowly up around them, while the elder of the two men—Mr. Coggins, beyond a doubt—dealt out hundred-lire notes to the porters, all of whom said that wasn't enough. The Coggins girl's slip was too long; she was holding a tennis racket in a wooden press. She looked as if she had just got off the train for summer camp. Her mother had put on one white glove. The young man, Wilbourne, gloomy in a tropical-weight tan suit, seemed hung over. Was this Mrs. Wilbourne sprinting up from behind, her hand to her brow as if she had forgotten something? But it was somebody else, a dark girl who ran off crying "Oh, Eleanor!" Mr. Coggins had greying hair that stood up in a two-weeks-old bristle. His lips were struggling with a language he believed he knew well. He understood opera, didn't he? "Scusatemi, per favore. . . ."

Martha hated to break this moment, for once they saw her, they would never be quite like this again. "Are you, by any chance, the Coggins'?" They were. How thrilled they were, how instantly relieved. They had been expecting her, but had not known where to look. It was all open and friendly beyond measure. Martha became exhilarated, and felt how really nice Americans were. So the group formed instantly and began to move forward together. "Taxi! Taxi!" It was a word everyone knew. . . .

Two weeks later George Hartwell rang them up. They had crossed Italy by then and had reached—he had guessed it—Venice. How was it going?

"Well, fine," Martha said. "It's mainly the Coggins'. Mrs. Wilbourne couldn't afford to come and stayed behind. She's flying out to Rome in a week or so. George, did you ever know an economist who didn't have money problems?"

He chuckled.

"Mr. Wilbourne doesn't stay with us much. He goes off to visit industries, though God knows what he can learn with sign language. It's churches and museums for the Coggins'—they're taking culture straight."

"Should I come up and join you with the other car?" His conference was over in Florence; he was feeling responsible and wondering what to do.

"We managed okay with the baggage rack. They've shipped nearly everything ahead." She felt obscurely annoyed at being found. "How did you know where we were?"

"I remembered that pensione, that little palace you like. . . ."

It was indeed, the pensione in Venice, a building like a private palace. It had once been some foreign embassy, and still kept its own walled campo, paved in smooth flagstones, ornamented with pots of flowers, boxed shrubs and bougainvillea. The tall formal windows opened on a small outdoor restaurant. "You mean we get all this and two meals a day?" Mr. Coggins was incredulous. "And all for six thousand lire each," chanted Mrs. Coggins, who was by now a sort of chorus. That was the first day. Jim Wilbourne, angrily complaining about some overcharge on the launch from the station, joined them from Padova just in time for a drink before dinner, and they felt reunited, eating out in the open with the sound of water, by candlelight. They decided to stay on for a day or two.

One afternoon they went out to the Lido—all, that is, except Martha, who had decided she would spend the time by herself, revisiting one or two of the galleries. When she came out of Tintoretto's Scuola into the quiet campo where the broad shadow of a church fell coolly (had everyone in Venice gone to the Lido?), there in a sunlit angle, a man, with a leather briefcase but no apparent business, stood watching. The campo, the entire area, all of Venice, indeed, seemed entirely deserted. There had been no one else in the gallery but the ticket seller—no guide or guard—and even he seemed to have disappeared. The man with the briefcase held a lighted cigarette in his free hand, a loosely packed nazionale, no doubt, for the smoke came gushing out into the still air. When he saw Martha pause and look at him, he suddenly flung both arms wide and shouted, "Signora, signora! Che vuol fa', che vuol fa'?" "I don't know," Martha answered. "Non so." "Something has gone wrong!" he shouted across the campo, waving the briefcase and the cigarette. "Somewhere in this world there has been a terrible mistake! In questo mondo c'è stato un terrible errore!"

Martha walked away to the nearest canal and took a gondola. Mad people show up all over Italy in the summer; they walk the streets saying exactly what they think, but this was not like that: it was only sciròcco. The air was heavy. She remembered Tintoretto's contorted figures with some desire to relax and straighten them out, and the cry from the man with the briefcase, comic and rather awful at once, swept through and shook her.

Already the sky was beginning to haze over. On a clothesline hung behind an apartment building, a faded red cloth like a curtain or a small sail, stirred langourously, as though breathing in the heat itself. The boat's upcurving metal prow speared free, swinging into the Grand Canal. Even here the traffic was light; the swell from a passing vaporetto broke darkly, rocking the gondola in a leaden way.

At dinner everyone was silent. Jim Wilbourne ate very little and that with his elbow propped beside his plate, Martha judged that the Coggins' bored him;

they seemed another order of creature from himself. Some days before he had wanted to know what Italian kitchen appliances were like. The kind of apartment he wanted in Rome absorbed him.

Jean Coggins, who had sunburned the arches of both feet at the Lido, looked about to cry when her mother said sharply: "If you insist on having wine, you could at least try not to spill it." Mr. Coggins, whose brow was blistered, sent back his soup which was cold, and got a second bowl, also cold.

To Martha the silence was welcome, for always before when gathered together, they had done nothing but ask her about the country—politics, religion, economics, no end of things. She was glad they had at last run down, like clocks, and that they could find themselves after dinner and coffee out in the back courtyard because some fiddlers had happened to pass. The guests began to dance, first with one another, then with strangers, then back to known faces again. When the music turned to a frantic little waltz, Jim Wilbourne stumbled twice, laughed and apologized, and led Martha to a bench near the wall, where they were flanked on either side by stone jars of verbena.

"I'm so in love with that girl," he said.

Martha was startled. What girl? The waitress, one of the guests, who? There wasn't any girl but the Coggins girl, and this she couldn't believe. Yet she felt as the guide on a tour must feel on first noticing that no one is any longer paying attention to cathedrals, châteaux, battlefields, stained glass or the monuments in the square.

Jim Wilbourne offered her a cigarette, which she took. He lighted it, and one for himself.

"Out at the Lido this afternoon," he went pleasantly on, "she got up to go in the surf. Her mother said, 'You're getting too fat, dear. Your suit is getting too small.' For once I could agree wholeheartedly with Mrs. Coggins."

So then it was Jean Coggins. "But she's only a kid," Martha protested.

"That's what I thought. I was ten days on that damn boat and that's what I thought too. Then I caught on that she only looks like a kid because her parents are along. She's nineteen, actually. And rather advanced," he drily added.

"But when—?" Martha exclaimed. "I've never seen you near each other."

"That's strange," said Jim Wilbourne.

She almost laughed aloud to think how they had so quickly learned to walk through walls; she felt herself to be reasonably observant, quite alert, in fact. But she was also put out—she and George Hartwell were not really delighted to have Americans who leaped into la dolce vita the moment the boat docked—if not, in fact, the moment they embarked. She got up and walked to the wall where she stood looking over the edge into the narrow canal beneath. From under the white bridge a boat went slowly past, a couple curled inside; its motor was cut down to the last notch, and it barely purred through the water. Before Jim Wilbourne came to stand beside her, the boat had slipped into the shadows.

"Italy always has this romantic impact," Martha began. "You have to take into account that the scene, the atmosphere—"

"Generalizations," Jim Wilbourne teased her, quoting something she was fond of saying, "are to be avoided."

"No, it's true," she protested. "After a year or so here, one starts dreaming of hamburgers and milkshakes."

"Indeed?" He flicked his cigarette into the water and turned, his vision drawn back to where Jean Coggins was dancing with the proprietor's son Alfredo, the boy who kept the desk. Her skirts were shorter, her heels higher, her hair, a shambles on her return from the beach, had been brushed and drawn back. She had put on weight, as her mother said, and she did, to Martha's surprise, look lovely.

Martha, who disliked feeling responsible for people,

toyed with the idea of seeking the elder Coggins and hinting at what she knew, but there in the faraway shadows, around and around a big oleander pot, the Coggins' were dancing cheek to cheek. Richard Coggins accomplished a daring twirl; Mrs. Coggins smiled. The two grubby musicans, with accordion and fiddle, who had brought an empty fiasco and offered to play for wine and tips, had not even paused for breath for an hour. They could go on like this all evening.

Sciròcco, Martha thought, deciding to blame everything on the weather.

She slipped away, walking inside the broad dimly lit hall of the pensione. It looked shadowy and lovely there, its wide doors at either end thrown open to the heavy night. On the beamed ceiling reflections from water were always flickering, breathing, changing. Behind the desk a low light burned, and the proprietor, a tubby shrewd-faced man, was bending over one of his folio-sized account books. He had told Martha that the pensione was owned by a Viennese lady, who came there unannounced twice a year. She might descend on him, like the angel Gabriel, he had said, at any moment. So he kept his nose to his figures, but now, as Martha went by on her thoughtful way upstairs, he looked up.

"Ah, signora," he said, "there's nothing to do about

it. Non c'è niente da fare." But what he meant, if anything, was not clear.

She heard the lapping of tiny waves from everywhere, and through a window saw the flowers against the wall, hanging half closed and dark as wine.

3

In Piazza San Marco where she went the morning after with some idea of keeping her skirts clear of any complications, Jim Wilbourne nevertheless appeared and spotted her. Through hundreds of tables and chairs, he wove as straight a line toward her as possible, sat down and ordered, of all things, gelato. He was wearing dark glasses as large as a pair of windshields, and he dropped off at once into a well of conversation—he must have enjoyed college, Martha thought. The scarcely concealed fascism of Italy troubled him; how were they ever to bring themselves out into democracy?

"Quite a number have jumped completely over democracy," Martha said.

"I simply cannot believe," he pursued, trying to light a cigarette with any number of little wax matches, until Martha gave him her lighter, "that these people are abstract enough to be good Communists. Or Democrats either, for that matter. I think when the Marshall Plan came along they just wanted to eat, and here they are on our side."

"Oh, I really doubt they're so unaware as you think," Martha said. "The idea of the simple-hearted Italian—not even English tourists think that any more."

"I don't so much mean simple, as practical, shrewd, mainly a surface life. What would happen, say, if this city turned Communist right now? Would one Venetian think of hauling the bones of St. Mark out of the cathedral and dumping them in the lagoon? I just can't see it."

"The Coggins' seem to like everything just the way it is," Martha laughed.

"Do you see that character as I do? As long as Richard Coggins can hear some ragazzo go by whistling 'O soave fanciulla,' he's gone to paradise for the afternoon. The more ragged the ragazzo is, the better he likes it. I have two blind spots; want to know them? Opera and religious art. A million churches in this country and quite likely I'm not going to like a single one of them."

"So no wonder you keep escaping us."

"Oh, it's been pleasant enough; you've done your best to keep us happy. And then, there's daughter Jean—" He paused, adding, "Don't get me wrong," though she had no idea what that meant. By now he was eating through a mountain of ice cream, striped with caramel and chocolate, piled with whipped cream and speared with wafers.

"The Coggins' are going down to Rome tomorrow," he went on. "As you know they've got this meeting with Coggins' opposite number, somebody who's going to the States to tell us all about jazz."

"I ought to know about it," Martha said. "I went to enough trouble to set it up. Anyway, it's chamber music, not jazz."

"Okay, Mrs. Ingram. So you'll get me straightened out some day; keep at it. Anyway, I wondered if maybe you wouldn't stay on a day or so, with Jean and me. She thought it would be a good idea; we could all go to the Lido."

"That might be fun," said Martha.

"If you're worried about the Coggins'—well, don't. Him and his bloody opera plots. Ketchup all over the stage, women's heads bellowing out of sacks. Is he serious? Those people were born to be deceived."

"The real hitch for me is that I have a schedule back in Rome. I only made this trip to please my boss."

"It can't be all that important," he pursued, though it was obvious to her that by actually mentioning deception he had spoiled it all.

"Anyway," she pointed out gently, "in this weather the water will be no good at all for swimming. There's sure to be a lot of rain."

"How nice to know so much."

She maneuvered easily, but the fact was he puzzled her. Are they all turning out like this, she wondered, all of them back there? Yet he consistently gained her attention, if that was what he wanted; she had found him attractive from the start, though she had assumed he was accustomed to creating this sort of reaction, and would not have thought it remarkable if he noticed at all. As for herself, she wanted only to place a face value on him. Tanned, solid, tall, dressed even to his watchband with a sort of classical American sense of selection, he was like something hand-picked for export; if you looked behind his ear you might find something to that effect stamped there. He was very much the sort who showed up in ten years leading a group of congressmen by the nose and telling them what to look for and where, though when on home leave she might encounter him even before that, being interviewed on some TV show. It would be like him to leap out at me, right in a friend's living room, she thought. And when he had appeared in

Venice a few evenings back, she had been looking toward the bridge he crossed to reach them and had seen him mount up angrily, suddenly, against the horizonless air. He gave her then, and fleetingly at other times as well, the impression of being seen in double, as people always do who carry their own image in their heads.

"How can you smoke and eat ice cream at once?" she asked him.

He stopped, both hands, with spoon and cigarette, in air. He looked from one to the other. "Funny. I didn't know I was." He dropped the cigarette at once, smashing it out carefully.

"I've been wondering how to tell you this," he said, still looking down, but straightening as he finished. "It just happens that I seem to know your former husband rather well."

The bright level surface between them on which she had, in her own way, been enjoying the odd sort of quarrel they had been having, tilted and she slid definitively, her heart plunging downward. So another one had arrived.

"Why didn't you say so before?" she asked him.

"It isn't so easy to say, especially if—"

"If you have a message," she filled in.

She sat looking out at the square. It had filled with tourists, mainly Germans moving in a slow, solemn, counterclockwise procession, ponderous, disorderly, unattractive, as though under tribal orders to see everything. There were the pigeons, more mechanical still, with their wound-up motions, purple feet and jewel-set eyes. And then there was a person, all but visible, right at home in Venice, moving diagonally across the great colonnaded ellipse of the piazza, head down, noticing no one, big shoulders hunched forward under his old tasteless tweed jacket, grey-black hair grizzled at the nape. He was going to the corner drugstore, somewhere near East 71st and Madison. The smell of a late New York summer—just a morning hint of fall—was moving with him, strong enough to dispel the scent of European cigarettes, the summer-creeping reek of the back canals. He would spread books on the counter, stir coffee without looking at it, clumsily allow the bit of lettuce to drop from his sandwich.

"Not so much a message," Jim Wilbourne said.

"You see, people are always turning up when I least expect them!" She longed now simply not to sound helpless.

"Oh, then," he said, in a relieved voice, "you must already know about the accident."

"Accident!" She started like a quiet, lovely insect into which someone has suddenly stabbed a pin; her wings quivered; her eyes were fixed.

"Oh my God, now I've done it!" She tried twice to speak but failed and the voice below the green mask soon continued: "I think he's all right now."

"Oh. . . . Then nothing serious happened—" She drew a shaky breath.

Jim Wilbourne glanced out across the square. "There was some doubt about his being able to walk, but I think—" He broke off again, tentative, mysteriously cold.

Martha stirred compulsively, as though to shake herself free of whatever net had fallen over her. In doing so, her knee struck the little table, rattling the cups and spoons. She remembered the letter on the table in Rome, and the emptiness of the envelope was now her own. "He was always a completely awful driver," she was presently able to continue. "Go on, now you've started. Tell me the rest."

Were they reading lines to each other? Nothing, even turning the table completely over, bringing three waiters rushing down upon them with long arguments about paying for the glassware, would have quite restored her bearings, or loosed her from this cold current into which he seemed deliberately to have plunged them both. "Tell me," she insisted.

His vision seemed, behind the glasses, to pass her own.

"Oh, it wasn't a driving accident. But who should tell you this?—it's not my business to. He was out hunting with one of his patients, up in the Berkshires. I never thought that aspect of it made too much sense—well—to take a mental patient hunting, that is. Almost like an experiment, just to see if he'd do it to you on purpose. I never meant to get into all this. But since he is okay now, you naturally will be relieved to know—"

The entire piazza, thickening steadily in the closing weather, had become a total wet-grey illusion. "This isn't Gordon Ingram," Martha said. "It can't be."

"Gordon? No, Donald Ingram. The psychologist, you know. My wife studied with him at Barnard. Well, he does have an ex-wife in Italy. It was just that we were sure—"

Martha was really angry now. "I think you invented the whole thing!" She had not quite lost control. Sparing herself nothing, she had hoped, as though striking off a mask, to find something unequivocal and human facing her, to lose the sensation of conversing with a paper advertisement for shirts and whiskey.

"No, honestly. Quite sincerely, I promise you. It was just a natural mistake."

If there was a person back of the glasses, she had missed him completely. She was not going to succeed in confronting him with anything, for his voice, with as much sameness as a record, went on, "—a natural mistake."

Well, she supposed it was true. She sat looking down into the treacly dregs of espresso in her cup, into which a drop or two of the oppressive mist occasionally distilled and twinkled. She gathered up her bag, lighter, a couple of packages including a glass trinket and a book she had bought for a friend, and got up to leave.

Jim Wilbourne leaped to his feet. He was halted by the waiter, who had arisen from nowhere to demand payment. Now he was running after her. "Wait!"

She turned. "If I don't see you . . . I may take the train down, to stop off in. . . ."

Just as he reached her a whole family of German tourists walked straight into him, knocking off his green glasses. Martha had the startling impression that an entirely new face had leaped into place before her, in quick substitution for the one she had been across from at the table. It was even saying different things: his tone now openly challenged her: "So you won't?" "No." "Not for even a day?" "Exactly."

Their faces, contesting, seemed for an instant larger than life; yet she could remember, recalling the exchange, no further words than that, and the moment must have faded quickly, for in retrospect it seemed telescoped and distant in the vast sweep of San Marco. Jim Wilbourne was backing away as though in retreat, and Martha stood holding her packages while two pigeons at her feet plucked at the smashed bits of his glasses. There was no weakest blot of sun and she wandered out of the square into the narrow labyrinth of Venice where the lions had mildew on their whiskers and St. George slew the dragon on every passing well.

She had looked back once, in leaving the arcades, thinking she had left a camera on a chair, and had seen Jim Wilbourne with Jean Coggins, who must have been nearby all along. They were standing near the corner of the arcade, talking. The girl had a white scarf wrapped around her hair. The vision flickered, and was gone.

He would have been angry with me anyway, she told herself. The story was only an excuse, a pretext. But why should I have angered him?

She walked, moving sometimes with clumps and clots of people, at other times quite alone, beginning to settle and stabilize, to grow gentle once more after the turmoil, the anguish, which his outlandish mental leap at her had, like a depth charge, brought boiling up inside her. She took a certain view of herself: someone, not unusual, who had, with the total and deep sincerity of youth, made a mistake; now, the mistake paid for, agonizingly paid for, the only question was of finding a workable compromise with life. But now at this point did she have to learn that there was something in life which did not want her to have even that? The threat seemed distinctly to be hanging in the air, as thick as the threat of heavy weather.

I should have talked more with the man with the briefcase, she thought, for, far from being mad, he had got things exactly right. Perchè in questo mondo è stato veramente un errore terribile. Don't I really believe that Jim Wilbourne's errore terribile was deliberate? She had accused him of it, certainly, and she did believe it.

She had believed more than that, looking back. She had thought that he was simply stirring up the Jean Coggins romance to question her authority—but that was before she had actually seen the girl standing there.

Martha stopped and almost laughed aloud. She had been about to walk straight into a wall, an architectonic device painted upon it to suggest continuing depth where none existed. The laugh would have bounced back at her, perhaps from the false corridors, the steps and porticos and statuary of that very wall. Laughter was a healthy thought, nonetheless, which said that not so many things pertained to herself as she sometimes seemed determined to believe. And as she stood there a woman much older than herself, grey, but active and erect, walking with the easy long stride of Venetians, who are good at walking because they are always doing it, went past and entered a doorway, bearing a net of groceries—la spesa—in one hand. Just before she entered, she glanced up, and a cat uncurled itself from the column base near the entrance where it had been waiting, bounded past the woman's feet and entered the door in one soft flowing motion. The door closed.

Martha recalled her apartment in Rome; how easily and comfortably it closed about her once she had got past the place where the messages waited and, beyond, found the salotto empty and free. How quietly then she took out her work and spread it on the table, opened the shutters out to the terrace in summer, or bent in winter to light the fresh fire the maid always left.

A new season lay ahead. Perhaps the messages would begin to dwindle now, and not so many couriers would show up; time perhaps had no other result but the dissolution of things that existed, and after this something new came on. Martha, if she never had anything worth calling a new life, would have settled simply for a new silence. It would happen, she believed, when Gordon Ingram finally went back totally to his friends, who would convince him that if his young failure of a second wife ever existed, she had had no right to. (And let it even be true, she thought; if it makes him content, why, I'll believe it too.) She thought then of Jim Wilbourne and Jean Coggins, off somewhere together in the city's rich labyrinth.

Asking the direction of the Grand Canal from a young woman who was eating chocolate, she went off in the way she was told.

4

Sometime after four it began to rain—the city, more than ever like a grey-ghost ship, a hynoptic evocation, nodded into the thicker element. The rush and whisper of rain came from every distance. Inside, the air clung like cloth. The maids at the pensione hastened about closing the shutters; they set the restaurant up indoors and brought candles out to decorate the tables—Martha felt she was viewing a new stage-set, a change of scene. Like an opera almost, she thought, and at that moment, sure enough, here came the Coggins', skimming in together hand in hand through the rain. Now they were laughing together at the door and soon, from the desk, were appealing to her. "Have you seen Jean?"

She said she hadn't, but Jean herself came along not much later, walking alone through the rain. She had been sightseeing in a palace, she said, and had got lost when she left it. "You go right upstairs and take a hot bath," Mrs. Coggins said.

Jean went by, making wet tracks, and looking curiously at Martha, of whom she was somewhat in awe. Her foreign clothes, her long fair smoothly put-up hair, her intelligence, and near absence of make-up made her seem to Jean like a medieval lady in a painting. "I can't tell what she's thinking," she had complained to Jim Wilbourne. And he had said nothing at all.

The Coggins' called Martha aside and confided to her with shining eyes that they had experienced a most curious phenomenon since coming to Venice. They had been able to relive in great detail, vividly, their entire past lives. Martha, who could not think of anything worse, nodded, smiling. "How wonderful," she said. "Marvellous," they assured her.

In the heavy air Martha had all but dissolved, and went upstairs to take a nap. She left the two Coggins' murmuring below. Tomorrow they would all be in Rome; there would be the sun.

She slept and dreamed.

In the dream Gordon Ingram was standing along

some country road, in New England, among heavy summer trees, and saying, "You see, I have been severely injured in a hunting accident. I cannot come there; please understand that otherwise I would." He looked very young, like the young man in photographs she had seen of him, taken long before they met, standing in the sort of hiking clothes he must have worn in walking over Europe in days, vacations, the like of which would never come again. She was reaching out her hand and saying, as in a formal note to someone, "I sincerely regret . . . I deeply regret. . . ." It seemed the first thing they had had to talk about in many years; the first time in many years that he had spoken to her in his natural voice. The rain-coloured shadows collected and washed over the image and she half woke, then slept again, but could not summon up the dream. She remembered saying to herself, perhaps aloud, "What a strange city this is." For it lay like a great sleeping ear upon the water, resonant and intricate. All the while the rain poured vastly down and could be heard even while sleeping and dreaming, speaking one continuous voice.

In a half-daze she woke and dressed and went downstairs, and at the desk found a note for herself. Jim Wilbourne had just left; he had probably let in the ragged splash of water near the door. He had written a scribble to say that he would see them all in Rome. She crumpled the paper and dropped it in a waste-basket back of the desk. She tried to ring George Hartwell, but could not reach him; the line seemed muffled and gave her only a vague wavering sound. The operator, after a time, must have shut her off for the day. But she remembered that George had said once, one evening when he had drunk too much, that Americans never lose their experience abroad, they simply magnify it. "It's the old trick of grandfathers," he had said. "Before the fire they make little motions and big shadows dance on the wall. Europe is the wall the shadows dance on." His voice went with her for a step or two.

There was nothing to do till dinner and she went upstairs again. The smell of cigarettes hung stagnant in the upper hall and from somewhere a shutter banged in the shifting wind. She pursued stairways and long halls, passed alcoves and sudden windows. Everything was as dark as her dream had been when it faded. A lance had whistled past her ear, and the impression persisted that she moved in a house of death.

part

two

5

In *Rome* that fall she stopped herself just before telling a friend that her husband had been wounded in an accident. This was very odd, for the fall was bright and sane, and she was at the time nearly eclipsed in cleaning up a lot of George Hartwell's extra chores. The cultural effort had taken on new life that year; the lectures were well received, the social events congenial; pools, lakes, marshes of American good will were filling up everywhere, and all Italians, you would think at times, were eventually going to splash and mingle in them, and the world would never be the same again.

A letter from a lawyer came to Martha, suggesting a price for some property she had owned jointly with

Gordon Ingram. It should have been settled long before; it was only since they had gone so happily into it—this small wooded crook of land beside a stream in New York State—that she could never bear to discuss it. But why wouldn't he write me about it? she wondered. Why get somebody else? She sat with the letter and realized something: that if he had had an accident it would have been about here that it happened, right on this bit of land. There were some rocks and a stream below a slope, screened by maple trees.

At last she wrote: "Dear Gordon: Do take the property outright. I do not want any money for it. Will sign whatever transfer is necessary. Martha."

But he could not stand brief notes, simple transactions, direct generosities. Her motives now would suspend him for days. When people dealt with him too quickly, he always suspected either that he had made them too good an offer, or that they were trying to shake away from him; and so, suspicious, obscurely grieved, he would begin to do what he called considering their own good; he would feel it his duty to make a massive reevaluation; he would call all his friends. He would certainly call them all about Martha.

They had all discussed her to death anyway; for years she had interested them more, it seemed, than they interested themselves. They had split her up and eaten her, some an arm and some a neck and some the joints of her fingers.

Sitting at her desk on a Sunday morning, in sunlight, Martha pressed her palm to her brow. Should she mail the letter at all, or write to the lawyer instead, agreeing to everything, or write to her own lawyer to take it over? And must all life, finally defeated, turn itself over with a long expiring grateful sigh into the hands of lawyers? No, she thought with sudden force; I will keep it a personal matter if both of us have to be accidentally wounded. It is, after all, my life.

So in the end she wrote two letters, one to the lawyer and one to Gordon Ingram. Once, before she left the States for Italy, a year after her divorce, she had run squarely into him in New York, getting out of a taxi she had hailed, and before she could stop herself she had almost screamed, and that must have been terrible for him—poor Gordon. But she well knew that if she deceived herself by thinking she knew how he felt, she might act upon it, with sympathy, and trap herself, falling a victim of his pride.

It seemed to her in retrospect that while she debated her letter that Sunday morning, the sun went away; sensually, in recollection, she could almost feel it slipping from her hair, her cheek, her shoulder, and now Rome was deep in winter, with early dusks, blurred neon on the rush of shining streets. Tramontana, the wind from the mountains, struck bitterly, or heavy weather moved in from the sea; the great campagna around Rome became a dreary battlefield of contentious air, and one had to be sorry for the eager Americans, there for one year only, who now had to learn that a sunny, amiable, amusing, golden land had passed in one night into a dreary, damp, cold dungeon of a world where everybody was out to cheat them and none of them could get warm. Martha was used to it. She had been there several years and she liked it. Far stranger to her had been that sudden shift of weather in Venice, back in the summer. It had plunged her, like a trapdoor opening under her feet, into a well of thought she could not yet get out of. She must have been deeply in it the very day when, going home in an early dark after tea with friends, she had run into Jim Wilbourne.

She had seen the Wilbournes fairly often during the fall. Rita Wilbourne, though somewhat more flamboyant than Martha cared to think about—she wore chunky jewelry, bright green and corals, colored shoes —was energetic in getting to know people. She studied Italian, learned it quickly, and took up a hobby—she would make ceramics. It had been a Grand Idea and now it was beginning to be a Great Success. All one room of the Wilbourne apartment had become a studio. It exuded the smell of solvents and plasters.

There had been intermittent invitations. George and Grace Hartwell, the Wilbournes, and Martha Ingram often found that they had gravitated into the same corner at a party, or were ringing each other up to come over for supper on rainy Sundays. What did they talk about so much as the Coggins'?

Jean Coggins had a job in a glove shop on the Piazza di Spagna. About once a week, every young Italian in Rome made a point of coming in and buying gloves. Some did nothing but walk back and forth before the window for hours. The owner was having to expand.

Richard Coggins was the success of the entire cultural program. His Italian, once it quit rhyming like opera, was twice as fluent as anyone else's; he learned, he learned! He was invited—a great coup for the American image—to address the opera company in Milan. His lectures were packed and ended with cheers and cries. (Bravo! Bis, bis!) Oh, no one had ever furnished more party talk than the Coggins'. Yet there was something enviable about their success.

One night at the Wilbournes' apartment after dinner, Jim Wilbourne remarked: "Jean Coggins' effect on

Italian men began to happen the minute the boat docked. It was spontaneous combustion. Do you remember Venice, Martha?"

Martha looked puzzled. She shook her head. The trouble was she remembered nothing but Venice; it was a puzzle which had never worked out for her; what exactly did he mean?

"There was some boy who kept the desk—Alfredo, his name was."

"Oh, yes, the proprietor's son."

"What happened?" someone—Hartwell's wife—wanted to know.

"Well, they were hitting it off so well that she wanted me to persuade Martha—you must remember this, Martha—to stay on a day or so, so that her parents would let her stay too. The only catch was she didn't want me to mention Alfredo: it seems the Coggins' believe that Italian men are incorrigibly passionate or something. She nagged me until I promised to do it, but the only excuse I could think of was to say I was interested in her myself."

Everyone laughed. "So what happened?" they wanted to know.

"Well, I got nowhere with Martha. She got out of it very well."

"What did you say?" Hartwell asked her.

"I forget"—she let Jim Wilbourne finish his story.

"She said she'd like to stay on but she had some appointments or other—very grand she was."

Hartwell, after a hard week, had had a drink or two more than usual. He gave Martha a hug. "I love this girl."

"But I was in the dark myself," Martha protested. She soon followed Rita into the next room to look at her workshop.

"So she tried to be philosophic, which for a Coggins is something of a strain, to put it mildly. She went off in the rain with Alfredo, off in Venice somewhere, and called it a day."

"I wouldn't have thought these two colors would go at all," Martha said to Rita, who had joined her. "But you've made them work."

"Yes, but Italians are so bold with their colors. I think it must be something in the sunlight here—when there's any sun, of course." She picked up two sections, handle and basin, from an unfinished hors d'oeuvres dish. "You see, you wouldn't think that would do well, but I find the more I experiment—" Her bracelets jingled together as her hands moved. They were thin, quick, nervous hands with tinted nails. Grace Hartwell had told Martha that the Wilbournes were expecting a child. Why is George such a puritan? Martha wondered.

You'd think I'd struck a blow for freedom by keeping lovers apart.

"Did you, by any chance," Martha asked Rita, "know a Professor Ingram at Barnard?"

"Oh, yes, but not at Barnard. I went to Columbia. He teaches there occasionally, one semester every so often. Yes, I not only knew him, but we were sure for a time that you must be the former Mrs. Ingram. She's somewhere in Italy. It's odd your asking that."

"I'd just recalled when we were talking of Venice that Jim mentioned him to me there. And several other times," she lied, "people have assumed that he—I never met this person, of course."

"But beginning to feel you know him rather too well?"

"I also heard he had been in some sort of accident last summer. Did you know anything about that?"

"Oh, that must be another Ingram still. No, unless something happened just recently—"

The ceramics were laid out in a bare, chilly servant's room on a large makeshift table, strips of wallboard held up by a smaller table underneath and supported on either end by chairs. The effect was of a transferred American look, makeshift and practical, at no pains not to negate the parquet floor, a scrolled mirror now layered with cement dust. A small French écritoire had been pushed into a corner, and beside it, a gilded baroque angel holding a torch stood face to the wall. The room had probably been intended as a smoking or drawing room off the salotto. They had dined on frozen shrimp from the PX, and only in here with the ceramics was the odor escapable. Why would anyone buy frozen American shrimp in Italy? Martha had wanted to ask, but had not. It had been answered anyway, at dinner; Rita was afraid of the filth in the markets. But the markets were not filthy, Martha thought, murmuring how delicious it was.

"Hey, Martha!" Hartwell again.

"We're busy," Rita called.

"Information required," Grace Hartwell said.

"They always want you to tell them things, don't they?" said Rita, with a moment of woman's sympathy. "If I were you, I wouldn't."

Martha came to the doorway, her shawl tugged around her. Her hands felt cold. Hartwell was lighting his third cigar. Would he not, singlehanded, eventually drive out both shrimp and ceramics smell? "Martha, I thought sciròcco was a wind. Jim here says it's not. He says in Venice it's nothing but heavy weather. Now you settle it."

"I believe it's an African wind," she said, "and

causes storms all along the coasts, but sometimes the wind doesn't get as far as Venice, especially in the summer, so then you have heavy weather and rain."

Jim Wilbourne laughed. "You mean it is and it isn't."

"I guess that makes you both right," she agreed, and smiled.

All their faces were momentarily turned to her. There was some way, she realized, in which, in that moment, she drew them, the two men primarily, and because of the men, inevitably, the women as well. She would have as soon dropped at once whatever force this was, dropped it off like her shawl on the threshold and walked away. But to where? she wondered, To where? No one can abdicate the earth.

Yet she kept on wondering this in some corner of her mind until the night she ran into Jim Wilbourne, down in the low Renaissance quarter of the city, in the windy, misty, December cold. In brushing past they recognized each other, and for some reason, startled, she slipped on an uneven paving stone so that he caught her back from falling. Then he asked her into a café and they had a drink together. She felt she was seeing him after a long absence.

He had changed somewhat; she noticed it at once. He was paler than in Venice, no longer seemed so well turned-out; needed a better haircut, had a cold. He was complaining about Italian medicine; it was his wife's having a miscarriage only a week or so after their dinner party that had got them so sensitive to these matters. Martha thought how soon the bright young Americans began to look tarnished here. The Wilbournes had had some squabble with the landlord about their apartment. He had believed that Rita, who had begun to sell her ceramics, was obviously using the place for business purposes, so he drew up papers demanding either eviction or a larger rent. Martha had heard this through the grapevine, in the same way she had learned that there had been some disagreement with American friends about a car. All these were the familiar complications of Roman life, which only the Coggins' seemed to escape. *Their* landlord had dreamed of an opera career when young, and as a result brought them fresh cheeses from the country, goat's milk, ropes of sausages. The Wilbournes, stubbornly American, were running against the Italian grain, so of course everything was going wrong. Yet Jim Wilbourne did work hard; it was this that Hartwell always said, as though making up for something.

Jim Wilbourne asked her the name of the pensione where they had all stayed in Venice. A friend of his was going up. "But do you think they'd enjoy it this time of year?" she asked. "What's the matter, the weather?" The weather, obviously; she hardly needed, she thought, to nod. "I must be thinking of Verona." He frowned. "There was a big fireplace—?" She shook her head. "I don't think so."

The door of the café stuck on the way out; getting it to work, he gave her an odd smile. He walked along with her for about a block, then, saying something about somewhere he had to be, he turned abruptly and went back the other way.

She turned around in the cold misty street, looking after him. The street was long and narrow and completely deserted, the shop windows covered over with iron facings which had been bolted to the pavement. Almost involuntarily, she lifted her hand. "Wait!" She did not speak very loudly and it was a wonder he heard her at all. He did stop, however, and looked back.

She began to walk toward him, and presently he even came a step or two to meet her. She stood huddled in her dark coat. The damp got in everywhere. She shifted her feet on the cold wet stones. "It's a silly thing to ask—I keep meaning to mention it whenever I see you, then I always forget. Do you remember a conversation we had in Venice when you said that someone you knew named Ingram—you mistook him for my husband—had been shot in a hunting accident?"

"I had hoped you'd forgotten that. It was a hell of a conversation. The whole place was depressing: some start for a year in Europe." He did not exactly look at her, but past her in a manner so basically unsatisfactory to her she would have liked to complain about it. Then when he did look at her, her face, she realized, slanting up to him, must have become unconsciously strained. She laughed.

"I'm shivering in this cold. This is ridiculous, of course. I wouldn't have remembered it at all, but Rita mentioned it to me, not long ago—this same man, I mean. But what she said was that he never had any accident at all. Neither he nor anyone else she knew."

"Well?"

"Well, I simply wondered what the connection was. Why did you say it at all?"

"I must have got him confused with someone else."

"Oh, I see. Someone you know and she doesn't?"

He did not reply.

"Was that it?" she insisted.

"Lots of questions," he remarked, amusing himself, though he was not what she could call light about it. "I guess I just don't remember it so well as you."

"It was in San Marco, in Venice. You ran after me and broke your dark glasses and just after that Jean Coggins came there—to meet you."

Watching him was like looking up into a dark mirror, or trying to catch some definite figure embedded in glass. Yet his features were singularly without any motion at all. She had, as she had had before, the impression of a photographed face.

"Oh, yes, Jean Coggins. . . ." She thought for a moment he would not continue. "She wanted you to stay on, she got me to ask you. I told you that," he added, impatiently. "In fact, I went to some trouble to tell you. As for her coming there, I don't remember that—I don't think it happened."

A Lambretta sputtered behind her, turning with a cough into the narrow, resounding street. The echoes clapped, climbing up to the high tile eaves above them. Pools of rain, surfaced in the uneven paving, seamed and splashed. Jim Wilbourne and Martha Ingram stepped back into a shallow alcove against an iron door, where large white letters were painted, advertising the name of the shop. The roar mounted with an innocent force and turmoil which seemed close to drowning them, then it passed, faded, turned a corner. They both stepped back into the street.

"All this seems to have got on your mind in some sort

of way," Jim Wilbourne said. "Here, come on, I'll walk you home."

The damp chill had crept up to her ankles, but she did not stir, though he caught her elbow to urge her forward. Her private idea of him was beginning to form; namely, that he was a sort of habitual liar. He might, if this was correct, be incapable of telling the truth even when it would do him no shred of harm to do so, even when it might be better that way. Any exact nature of things he was called upon to reconstruct might seem always to escape him. Hartwell had called her in once about a mix-up which had involved Jim Wilbourne and she had said then that she thought he was absent-minded, but Hartwell protested, "That simply won't hold a thing like this." Then she said, "I don't think he would do anything to damage his work." They were, between them, she and Hartwell, aware of new Americans, newer than themselves, perhaps different, perhaps more nearly right, than they who had been "out here," "away from things" for longer. The feeling was that people, like models of humanity, might quickly become obsolete in some overruling set of American terms even now, beyond their knowledge or power, being drawn up; so their confidence grew weak before the solid advantage of the Wilbourne image. He was so definitely American-looking, while Hartwell had recently given in to shoes with pointed Italian toes which looked extremely odd on him, and Martha went habitually to Roman dress-makers and looked extremely well, though hardly Fifth Avenue. So with this thinking interchanged be-tween them, Hartwell agreed not to make an issue of the Wilbourne default, and let the matter slide.

Martha said to Jim Wilbourne, "Naturally it got on my mind. It concerned me, didn't it?"

"Not at all. It concerned me, Jean Coggins and a man you used to be married to."

She gave a laugh that did not sound altogether pleasant, even to herself. "A rather close relationship," she said. Rambling about in those half-dreams which Gordon Ingram's giant mahogany bed, like being lost on a limitless plateau with the same day's journey al-ways in prospect, seemed both to encourage and deny, she had often thought the relationship could be a lot closer, yet now she regretted most the times that it had been. She would have liked to extinguish those times not only out of memory but out of time itself.

They began to walk off together in her direction. She protested against being any trouble to him, but he did not seem to hear her, and soon he was walking ahead at a rapid, nervous pace she found hard to keep up with in her thin shoes. His long legs and narrow heels kept striking accurately down before her. The streets were narrow and dark and his raincoat went steadily on, as though its light colour cut a path for them.

"Jean Coggins," he told her with his short hoarse laugh, "has a lot of boy friends but never gets to bed with any of them. We found this out from the maid whose sister works for the family of one of the boys. She's a grand girl in topolinos, picnics, out among the tombs. She could probably make love in a sarcophagus. Her morals are well-defined, but what if she never gets over it?"

"How do her parents get along with all this?" Martha asked.

"Her parents," said Jim Wilbourne, "are still in Venice, dancing around a flower pot."

This was not only funny, but true; Martha often saw them there herself.

He slowed his step, letting her catch up even with him, and for a moment caught her hand. "Why do I always talk to you about Jean Coggins?"

"It does get monotonous," she admitted.

"I can't think why I do it. She's comical. All the Coggins' are comical."

"You told me you loved her. You're probably still trying to get out of that."

"I don't know. It was the Italian boy—"

"Yes, I know. Alfredo."

"I remember now I told her to ask you herself, about staying on in Venice, but she didn't have the nerve. She found you awe-inspiring, your intelligence, authority, something—I don't know. As for me, I had some sort of strong feeling for you, right from the first. I imagined you felt the same, but then—" He broke off, but added, rather drily, "Your attention was elsewhere. You seemed—enclosed."

She said nothing, walking, hearing their footfalls on the stones, and how sometimes the sound of them interlocked and sometimes not.

"I try not to think of myself at all," she ventured. And this was true; she would have put herself quite outside her own harsh, insistent desire for him, if this had been possible. As it was not, she meant simply to hold it aside.

"Well, you don't succeed," he said pleasantly. "Nobody does."

"You took that way of getting my attention by telling me that Gordon—that my husband—" Only to get that question out of the way! She felt she could get herself intellectually right, at least, and as for the rest— But striving with him to get it answered only drew her deeper in and her feeling mounted that it was no more possible to make him speak openly to her than to make an intelligent animal consent to converse.

"I kept trying to get out of it, once I started it," he reminded her. "But nothing seemed to work. I had some notion you were slipping away from me; you did it repeatedly—it was a question of whether anything on earth could reach you at all. On that peculiar day, the question seemed what you might call urgent."

"But even on a peculiar day," she argued, "to make up death like a parlor game—"

He stopped walking. "I didn't invent any death. You did—or seem to have."

It was true. Her heart filled up with dread. Not even her dream had mentioned death. The wildest leap of all had been her own.

"Oh, God!" she murmured. "Oh my God!" She stood before him, her head turned severely aside. They had reached the top of her street, and from the far end there came, in the narrow silence, the trickle of a commonplace little fountain. The mist, shifting, prickled sharply against her cheek. Some minutes back, from high up among the roofs and terraces, a cat had mewed, trapped on a high ledge.

He drew her in, quickly, easily, against him. The motion for them both was accurate beyond measure, and the high tension between them broke up almost at once. At its sudden departure, she gasped sharply. His arm still tightly around her, he brought her to her doorway

ignored; she found it about the same time as she located the key. "But you do see what I meant to say." Her hand lay urgently on his arm. "It's important to me to know you understand."

"I understand it isn't true. You'd never have called me back tonight if it hadn't been for what you call my miserable story in Venice. And you know that, Martha, don't you?" He gave her a demanding shake. "Denying it—that's no good."

"I know, I know, but I—" The words rushed out at last like a confession. She felt a deep pang of relief and was unable to finish what she had begun by way of protest. She felt shaken and outdone. All her life she had longed for some world of clear and open truth, reasonable and calm, a warm, untroubled radiance (the sort of thing that Gordon Ingram wrote about so well), but though she thirsted like the dying for it, it never appeared to her and she wondered if every human being was not surrounded by some dark and passionate presence, opaque and confusing, its face not ever to be discerned without enormous cost. The rush of her emotion had thrown her fully against him, and she disengaged herself slowly. He let her go.

"I never meant to injure you," he said at last. "It's only that—well, I suppose in this case it matters, keeping straight on things."

Straight! She almost burst out laughing. Well, she thought somewhat wearily, all her rush toward him brought to a complete stop, she supposed he *had* gone to some high degree of concentrated effort to keep her straight. As for the straight of *him,* it was such another question, it made her dizzy to think about it. The truth about even so slight an episode as the Coggins girl alone would have quite likely baffled a detective force. And where, for that matter, had he been going tonight? In a return to her native aristocratic detachment, she could not bring herself to ask him things like this; perhaps it was because she did not really want to know.

She turned, finding her key in her bag, and tucking her hair up with one hand, unlatched the door. It was a small winter- and night-time door cut within the larger portone, and sprang easily back so that she stepped inside the dimly lit interior at once. She looked back reluctantly to observe him. He had not pressed in behind her but stood as she had left him. It was only that one arm was thrown out against the door. The crumpled sleeve of his coat, the white inch of cuff, the set of his hand, pressed into her senses like the bite of a relief. His gaze, meeting hers, did not implore her for anything. His face was simply present, and would be, she recognized, as it had been for a long time now, present and closely with her whether she shut it out or not. From somewhere she had gained the strength to take it now, deliberately, whenever the moment came, between her two hands.

She nodded, and bending sideways to avoid the low frame, he stepped inside. The closing door made a soft definitive thud, echoing strongly within, but only once, dully, in the narrow street outside. She mounted the long stairs, proceeded through corridors and turnings, archways and landings. She did not look back or speak, but moved quietly on ahead of him.

She had lived a year at least, she thought, since running into him in the Via de' Portoghesi.

part

three

6

George Hartwell got the news in Milano. By then it was summer, summer even in Rome which he had left only two days ago to help maneuver the Milan office through a shake-up; and the weather finally pleased everyone. The old damp, closed medieval shrunken city, which had all but destroyed them all, had evaporated in one hour of this glorious new season. And what could have happened in it that was not gone with it? he wondered, and read the letter once more.

On Sunday morning he was driving there. It's the least I can do for her, he thought, just in case. In case of what? The road flickered up, the sea appeared and melted away and crashed in again. In case, in case, he thought, and soon might even make a song of it, and go bellowing as operatically as Richard Coggins all along the sea road south, past Santa Margherita, Porto Fino, with Tarquinia ahead and Santa Marinella . . . the plains, the mountains and the sea.

In some ways he wondered if it was a serious matter at all. Is any personal matter, he asked himself, a serious matter any longer? Isn't a personal matter simply a bug in the machine? Get rid of it as quickly as possible, or one of the rockets in your space capsule might jam. Push button C with all due reverence, for any other one will be your doom. The sea grew pink, then crimson, then a blue so deep and devastating he thought he would give up all considerations and sit out several days on a rock. Then life would change, if we would do that. If every other person, every other week. . . .

A Lambretta roared up out of a curve, all but shaving the paint from his left front fender. He did not slacken speed, but drove on. He was not going to go and sit on any rock, ever, not even if they dropped the bomb next week.

Martha Ingram, all this time, was serenely alone upon her terrace, drying her long hair in the sun. Observant as a cat in the morning still, she had just seen far down in the little square below, where the fountain twinkled, the last courier come and go, a rich little white-haired lady from Connecticut, some cousin or friend (was it?) of Gordon Ingram's—Martha could not remember her name. The sun stood at ten and a large daytime moon floated in the sky, pale, full-blown as a flower, it seemed a contrivance of the imaginary sort, fragilely mounted for effect. Was it because she could not remember the name that she had not gone to the door? The name, actually, had been called to her attention no earlier than yesterday, when a note had come, written from the lady's hotel—the Grand, of course, nothing less. (Martha had often thought that Gordon Ingram was in Rome and staying at the Grand, which would have suited him so; they had large fronded palms in the lobby, and the steps which broke the interior floor between the reception area and the lounge were so long you could never find the end of them.) Martha wondered what she had done with that note—she didn't know.

Just now, through the beautiful weather, an hour earlier in the summer morning the Italian messenger from the embassy had come with a dispatch case for her: she was to add a stack of reports for Hartwell and take them in the next morning. Well aware of the season, the Italian, whose name was Roberto, was amiable and conversant and invited her for an afternoon at the beach. He had his sister's car, he said, by way of recommendation, and had recently visited the States. Martha agreed the beach would be nice; she had got together with him on several minor problems recently and had found him astute. He was, in a pleasant way, a sort of social spy; he could tell an arrivato a mile off, and he knew ways of isolating, or deflecting, people.. If Hartwell had found some way of listening to someone like Roberto during the winter past, the Coggins' would not have leaped to such prominence in the cultural program that people now had the Americans all taped as opera lovers. So what Roberto was in turn going to want . . . questions like that flowed along easily with Roman life; they were what it was about. She thought of that gently sparkling sea and what a slow progress she had made toward it through heavy weather a year ago, back when it all began.

Going out, Roberto passed by the porter and the little lady in blue. Martha could hear by leaning over the terrace that the porter (whom she had bribed) was saying over and over: "La Signora Ingram non c'è . . . la Signora Ingram è fuori Roma." Roberto stopped by the fountain; turning swiftly, he seemed to stamp himself with a kind of ease on his native air. "Si, si, c'è . . . la signora c'è . . . l'ho appena vista." Then, catching some glance from the porter, he retreated.

"O, scusi . . . uno sbaglio. . . ." He turned, a little grey Fiat, the sister's car, no doubt, his goal, but the little lady shot after him, quick as a rabbit. She caught his sleeve. "I am looking for Mrs. Ingram. She lives here. Now would you be so kind." "Non parlo inglese, signora. Mi dispiace. . . ." How quickly, Martha thought, they did solidify. She had always, from the first, had some knack of getting them on her side. But was it fair that poor little lady friends of the family should get the runaround? Le prendono in giro, Martha thought. They are leading her in a circle. A little more and she would go down and open the door, come what might.

She never saw any friends, messengers, from the States any more. She never read her mail. And when the little lady looked up, she ducked cleverly behind the parapet of the terrace, bringing her hair, which she had just shaken damp from the wet scarf to dry, down with her. She loved the warmth on the back of her neck, the sun's heat reaching to the roots of her hair, through the fabric of her dress. Who would leave it for a minute to descend three stone flights that still smelled like winter?

So the rich lady cousin went away in her fitted blue summer coat with the funny squat legs V-ing down from the broad behind into the tiny feet in their specially ordered shoes. What a world of shopping, the kind these ladies did, came back to Martha as she watched her go. And there was her loud English to the porter (the louder we speak the more chance we have), and then for the sweeter part, her brave attempt at Italian: "Voglio parlare con la Signora Ingram, per cortesia." It was as if someone had said that if the lady's duty lay in climbing a mountain at once, she would not even have stopped to change clothes.

The porter was not touched in the least. "No, signora. La Signora Ingram non c'è. L'appartamento è vuoto." They went on and on, their voices in counterpoint, echoing in the wide-open hallways below, now touching the fountain, now climbing to the terrace. If I could think of her name, Martha thought, I might weaken and let her in. Surely she has nothing to do with, knows nothing about, the property in New York State which they must have got me to sign something in regard to or they would not now be so determined to get me to sign something releasing it. You would think they had found a deposit of gold and diamonds six inches beneath the soil, though it is quite possible that I am holding up a real estate development. Who can tell what goes on back in that green dream across the Atlantic?

The porter kindly called a cab. Now he would earn two ways—the tip from the lady, and Martha's bribe. All he had to do was be as adamant as a barred door, which was his true nature anyway. The lady rode off in her hat of blue-dyed feathers with the tight veil, fitting sleekly as it had been carefully planned to do, over her white hair, her two million wrinkles. She held her neck up straight, giving orders to the driver, an indomitable little white duck.

If I could have thought of her name, I would have let her in, thought Martha, as the cab disappeared from the square. She wasn't as bad as the rest of them, I do remember that. Martha knew too, by the slight degree of feeling by which even mad people recognize character, as though fingers upon a fine string in the dark had discovered a knot in it, that the lady in blue was not indulging in ugly suspicions as to if and why lies had been told her. She was saying that she simply did not know. That was all.

Oh, mythical bird, vanishing American lady! She had been, Martha felt certain, the last courier.

Martha picked up her hairbrush and, drawing her chair close to the edge of the terrace, she began to brush her hair. The bells had begun to ring, and she had put her hair up when George Hartwell drew up in the square below, hot and rumpled and jaded, hitching up the handbrake sharply. So I was right to have the papers ready for him, Martha thought, but it wasn't especially the papers he had come there for. He tossed his hat aside and sat down in the sun.

He held out a letter to her, though it had come to him. "Your sister says you don't answer your mail," he told her, stirring the coffee she brought him. "She also wants you to know that Gordon Ingram is very sick. He is in New York Hospital."

"I haven't answered much mail recently," Martha admitted. "I've scarcely read my mail at all."

A long silence grew up between them. Hartwell's wife was in the States attending their son's graduation from prep school in Massachusetts. Everyone had begun to be displaced. The Wilbournes were gone, Jim to take a job on some new economic council for advising private industry, and Rita to open a ceramics shop, having shipped loads of material, not quite legally, through embassy channels. They had left their flat in a mess, having sneaked out unexpectedly three days early: Hartwell still had calls from the landlord. The parquet was ruined, the mirrors. . . .

How was it that the sun seemed literally to warm one's heart? Hartwell now thought kindly of Martha Ingram's husband for the first time in his life. The poor old bastard, was what he thought. A man that age. Quite likely he's dying.

"So will you consider going there?" he asked her. "It can be arranged."

In the sun her hair shimmered like a fine web. Hartwell had once said about Martha Ingram when he was drunk, "Being from Springfield, Missouri, I am moved by women with grave grey eyes," which, as everyone told him, made no sense at all. It was a flight that failed. He had had some reference to his mother, aunt, some old magazine picture, or advertisement, maybe, showing a lady who wore her long hair up, face partly turned aside, serious and quiet. It was his way of worrying out loud. For his wife had speculated that there was undoubtedly a man in her life, but who? Hartwell used to think it over in the office alone and then wad paper up and hurl it at the wastebasket.

A slight movement just now of a curtain through one of the terrace windows made him think of Jim Wilbourne's even, somewhat longish, smoothly observant face, his nervous gesture of banging the heel of a resoled American shoe against a desk or chair leg when he talked, his cough and cigarettes and short hoarse laugh. Anybody, thought Hartwell, but Jim Wilbourne. Yet there she was, shining and fair, surfaced out of a long hard winter.

"Going there?" she repeated, as if he had mentioned a space ride. "It's nothing he's suggested. Don't tell me she said that."

"No," Hartwell admitted, "but look at it anyway. . . . You haven't even read it." She had taken it, but it was lying on her lap. When she moved, it slid to the terrace and she did not pick it up.

"But I know anyway," she said. "The last time I saw him was in Venice. He did not even look my way."

"Venice! Your husband was not in Venice," Hartwell corrected her, with a slightly chilly feeling.

She tucked one foot meditatively beneath her. "You see how crazy I am," she pointed out.

After some time, Hartwell said, "Intentionally crazy, I take it?"

"It's necessary," she finally replied.

At this Hartwell stopped drinking coffee, perhaps forever.

"What are you thinking?" she asked him.

"I think the weather is better," he said.

"That isn't what you think," she said gently, and gently too she went so far as to pick up the letter and place it—most untrustworthily—upon the table.

A small bell in a small church rang close by. It had a lovely clear sound and one actually looked about, expecting to see it, as though for a bird which had burst out singing.

"If only you could have got by without Wilbourne!" Hartwell cried, astonishing himself.

Martha built a pyramid out of burnt matches beside the milk pitcher. "He's gone. And anyway, what was it to you?"

"I didn't like him," said Hartwell arbitrarily. "This has happened before. It's nothing new. Those tall young men. . . ." It had happened all his life, in fact; he never having been one of them. At Harvard he had seen them, in the clothes of that day, older, of course, than himself, their strong easy step moving down corridors; and at Oxford, English tall with heavier bone structure, their big knees ruddy and tough in the blear cold. Now they were younger and would be younger still, but the story was still the same. "One expects such brilliance, and what happens? A moderately adequate work program, someone dear to me damaged"—she gave him a glance but did not stop him—"and now this headache of an apartment going on and on into the summer."

They had wrecked their apartment when they left, Jim and Rita Wilbourne. The parquet, the mirrors, the plumbing, the furniture. It was a vengeance on the landlord whose nature was infernal, and who had made their life a grating misery for the whole year. Now Hartwell had to listen to the landlord; he came once or twice a week to Hartwell's office; he would come tomorrow. "Signor console, deve capire che sono un uomo giusto e gentile. . . . You must understand I am a just and honorable man." The world was smeared and damaged, and Martha's craziness obsessed him, the more because she having completed herself he was in some ways crazier than she, else why would he let the landlord in for these interminable visits complaining of something which he could be said to be responsible for only in the vague sense of directing an American program in which Jim Wilbourne had, for a short time, taken part?

"You are linking me, George," she half-teased him, "to what the Wilbournes did to the landlord. Is that reasonable?"

"No, it isn't. It isn't reasonable at all. It just happens to be the truth, that's all. And anyway, you didn't see it—you didn't get the guided tour after they carried out the crime and ran away to Naples in the night. Carelessness is one thing, disorder left by people who aren't so tidy, something not at all nice about it, smelly maybe, but still human. But Rita and Jim Wilbourne had taken hammers, crowbars, scissors . . . !" He had begun, somewhat ludicrously, to shout.

Martha thought it was time somebody repaid a Roman landlord in kind, though anything short of crucifixion seemed genteel, but even to think of a Roman landlord seemed out of place in the timeless, non-bitterness of a Sunday morning full of sun.

"If he found that was the only way to get even," she said, "there may even have been some logic in it. I'm sure he got no more than even, and maybe no less. You forget he was an economist, so that might have something to do with the way he felt; I really don't pretend to know."

"I'm sure you would know more than I would," Hartwell said, somewhat recovering himself.

"I know he was the only one who could deal with Gordon Ingram—I do know that. But I never thought of him as smashing apartments up, though now that you mention it—"

The little church bell stopped ringing about then, and she wondered at Hartwell, this stupor of moral horror in his face, and predicted, the instant before he did it, that he would ask for a drink. She went and got it, drifting free and anchorless through her apartment, then going off to rearrange some flower pots, having no more ties than a mobile, invisibly suspended in the sun. Yet she was kind enough to reassure him. "If my judgment of him is worth anything, he seemed more quiet than not."

"Quietly murderous?" Hartwell murmured and fell into the scotch with a sigh.

She had to recognize, for by turning her head she could even see what made a space for itself rather constantly in her mind—how the room just beyond the tall windows onto the terrace looked now. They would have both known a long chain of rooms like that from childhood on, known their quiet, with shadowy corners and silent chairs and pictures that look only at one another, ornaments of no earthly connection to anything one knows about or can remember, and known too the reason for their precise quality, even down to the slow wind of dust motes in the thin slant of winter sun, the cool rest the marble has in summer, and the small light of the lamps: the reason being that somebody has been got rid of in them. In spite of her, their thoughts, like profiles in a modern painting, merged and coalesced: she appeared as one of a long line of women who have rooms like this: invariably handsome, well-dressed, detached, goalless, they have struck at life where it lived, unnaturally, because it grew unbearable.

He recalled from his long lost Missouri days, various women, their features indistinct, but their spirits clear to transparency, who lived in shady white houses with green latticework under the porch where the land sloped away. In varying degrees of poverty and wealth, they gave up their lives day by day, like sand running through a visible hourglass, to some trembling cross old father or invalid brother or failure of a husband or marvellously distorted and deeply loved child. But out and away from this monotony, they ranged far and wide among friends of the town, accepted, beloved, understood, praised. He saw them shift through that lost world with the sureness of angels, and though he said to himself it was lost, the thought occurred to him that it was perhaps only himself that was lost to it; for certainly it was there still: what made him think it wasn't? It was still there and going on, and repeating moreover its one relentlessly beautiful message, that you had to stand what you couldn't stand, or else you couldn't live at all. And for the first time it came to him that Martha Ingram did not, any longer, exist. He felt a pang of missing her, as though sometime back somebody had come in the office and told him the bad news and he had done all the decent things.

Whereupon she looked at him, reflectively, through the sun, and all the fabric of his fantasy crumbled. At least in the warm intelligent effigy of the flesh she was still there and still able to get through to him. She was all but pointing out to him that he didn't really know, how could he know just how it was? It was inhuman; it was monstrous—that was the first thing to know. Therefore, who was to say what she had or hadn't had the right to do about it?

7

As *to* whether or not she was really there any more, she could have said that she had simply become the winter past. Its positive motion against her, which seemed at times as blindly relentless as a natural force breaking up her own life, would always be with her. But it could not, unlike a natural force, ever be forgotten, for human faces had appeared in it and voices had cried to her, human motion had struck her down, and by these things, grasped at, sometimes only half understood, she had been changed for good, and could never escape them. It had been a definitive season.

But why George Hartwell now had to rush back into its devastating glooms and vapours, the flicker of its firelights, and quick gasps of its passions, so grotesquely lighted up in shadow play against the walls of his good and gentle heart—that she could not say. She did not really want to say. He seemed distant to her. She was fond of him. She could not have been any more or less than that if he had wanted her to, and he would never say so if he did, even, she supposed, to himself. She could, however, indulge him. He had his curiosity, so much a part of his affection—she could honor both by letting him in on things. She doubted if she would ever go so far as to say very much about the evening she had run into Jim Wilbourne on the Via de' Portoghesi, but in a way by just recalling it, it could be in some way shared by George Hartwell's openness in her direction, which she might have been leaning over to pat on the head, like a house pet. But then, of course, he would want to get past all that as hastily as possible, and on to the next thing, the next stone in her private torrent, and she guessed, looking back that that would have been the Boston lawyer. In January, wasn't it?

Yes, she could share that with George. She could even tell him about it, for she would not forget a single detail of it, even down to the grey suit the lawyer was wearing. He was all grey, in fact, all over, even to his cuff links, hair, and tie, and his name was grey as well—Bartram

Herbert. He was a close friend of Gordon Ingram's. She had known him for years.

He flew in in the afternoon, to Ciampino, just as his telegram had said he would. She did not meet the plane, and had even decided that she would leave the city for Naples, but unable to make herself do so, showed up exactly where he had asked her to, the Flora lobby near the Porta Pinciana. She even arrived on the exact hour, clasped his hand with a pale smile and turned her chilly cheek for a token kiss. He took her down to have a drink with him in the bar. Next he ordered a cab to Ranieri's (had he reserved by cable, she wondered?), which is an old-fashioned Roman restaurant where the carpets sink deeply in and the soft chandeliers swing low and the waiters murmur in French, bending at Monsieur's elbow, and he said (this being the kind of place his voice was best adapted to), "Gordon feels some income should be set up from the land for you. It is on his conscience because you may remember that some of your parents' legacy went into the original purchase; it was not noted in the deed of sale and indeed could not be; this is only a matter of personal conscience, as I'm sure you must appreciate correctly."

She was wearing a stern black suit and noticed, in a discreet but enormous mirror in a heavy frame, how pale she looked, though perhaps it was only the lighting, how subdued she sat, almost clipped out with scissors. She watched the neat insertion of his pointed spoon in the melon he had discovered on the menu and was now enjoying, and longed to say, "But you and Gordon were directors in that trust company that failed in the crash—I heard all about it—and somehow you never got precisely ruined, though of course ruined was the word you used for yourself but it was never visible." But she did not. She wondered if it was not too easy to suspect dishonesty where people are really only loyally seconding one another's ideas, echoing one another's politics and views of humanity which sound despicable, only to prove their common ground of affection. Then she said, "I think the trouble with all these messages, these visitors and plans and letters and schemes, is that everyone is looking at things only as Gordon sees them." His glance was sheer genius. "Oh, not at all, my dear. If it's what you feel, why that's unfortunate, but certainly in Mrs. Herbert's—Ruth's—view and my own, you and Gordon were simply too dissimilar to manage a happy arrangement." Dissimilar! She tried desperately to keep the word from clanging in her head. Had Gordon really poisoned the dog, as she suspected? she wanted to ask, for certainly the vet had told her so, clear and round, and he had said, if you think I will stoop to so much as answer this degrading nonsense. The dog was not poisoned, they are either confused or are deliberately telling you something to cover some mistake on their own part. There was, of course, another word like dissimilar: incompatible. "I have often wondered, however, granting the fact that no one can really say what causes such desperate conditions in a marriage that divorce is the only way out—I have often wondered what I did to turn all Gordon's friends against me. Why did you hate me so much?"

"It looked that way to you, did it?" He took a small sip of French wine. "I can see how it might. We all felt, you see—protective of Gordon. He has meant, through the years, so much." "So you wanted him back to yourselves?" "There was some sort of reaction." "There certainly was," Martha agreed. "I wanted to love you," she added. "I'm sure we made it difficult for you," he admitted. "I, for one, was somewhat conscious of it at the time. I tried, in some way, do you remember, to make amends." "I remember," she said, "that you took me down to see the fish pond." "So I did." He smiled. "And wasn't that pleasant for you?" "Yes," she said, "but it was scarcely more than decent. You never said anything to let me know you saw the difficulties I was half drowning in, with everyone else." "Well, but wouldn't that have been disloyal to Gordon?"

There was the thin sound of his spoon touching down on the plate and she said, "I suppose now that this bit of land is turning out to have some value I have not heard about."

"There is no attempt afoot to give you less than every cent that could possibly be due you."

"I did not mean there was," she said. Good God! she thought, how old he makes me feel. "I only meant that I have a reasonable interest in business."

"Well, then, you may as well know that the area is being opened up as suburban property—quite in the junior executive line; maybe you aren't familiar with the term."

"Oh, yes."

"Has someone else got to you then?"

"Oh, no, it's only that I guessed that I was being treated rather well for there not to be better than average sums involved." I shouldn't have said that, she thought. Of course, I make them angry; they don't like it, of course, they don't like it, and why do I do it? "Listen," she said intensely, "I'm sorry. I never meant to—"

"You must remember, my dear, that Gordon only got interested in finance through having to manage property you were left with. He saw what a sorry mess things were in where you and your sister were concerned and he so interested himself that he could now earn fifty thousand a year as a market analyst, that is, if he cared to. Your sister Annette says she never goes to bed without thanking God for Gordon Ingram."

In Martha's view her sister Annette was a near illiterate who would have gone on comparing prices of soap powders if she had a million dollars. She felt a blind white tumult stir inside, the intellectual frustration, of always being—she could only think deliberately, but how was one to know it was—misunderstood.

"I think it's wonderful how well he manages money, but that wasn't the point of what I was saying."

"Why don't we take our coffee elsewhere, if you're agreeable." In the carrozza he hailed for them in the narrow empty street, he conversed intelligently about the city, telling her in the course of some chance recollection several things she didn't know. And in the carrozza she experienced the tug of motion as one doesn't in a car, and the easy sway of the wheels, the creak of leather. He handed her down in a comfortable way. "Well, and what a pleasant thing to do!" Moving her toward a quiet café, "Shall we just have some coffee here?"

How charming they would all be, she thought, if only one could utterly surrender the right ever to disagree with them. She wished she could have sat in the handsome bar, all white rococo and gilt, and bring him out on some old story or other: reminiscence, that was what they loved, but she had desperately to try once more, for the bar was teeming with Italians: he was all she had of America here.

"I only wish that someone would admit that a man can be as wonderful as a saint to everyone in the world, but behave like a tyrant to one person."

He gave her a quiet grey look. "I cannot see anything tyrannical about Gordon wishing you to have your share of this property settlement."

"I only want to be forgotten," she said.

"Surely a rather singular wish."

It was right there on the table that she signed it. She remembered the crash of the gun down by the stream's edge. The ink flowed easily from the pen. It was only, she thought, a question of money. His hands in receiving documents were extremely adept.

"There will of course be other papers," he said. "They will reach you through the mail."

8

And all this time in the thick or cutting weather of that winter she had been blown adrift about the city, usually going to put in a social appearance somewhere that the Hartwells didn't have time for, and when George saw her as he did see her once, driving by in his little car—she was on the Veneto—it gave him the odd sensation that all was not well. As if to confirm it she stopped still and laughed. The sight was pleasant, but the idea worrying; she had told him something even back that far about the Boston lawyer, whom he had actually seen her having cocktails with at the Flora, but, in the days that followed the laugh, he fell to wondering what his responsibility was. He recalled the sudden break in her walking there by the high wall just past the embassy, and the giant twin baroque cupids playing with a basin into which a fountain gently spilled, and thought that if Martha was in New York she would be swelling some psychiatrist's income by now, a thing he withdrew himself from even considering. He sat meditating evenings before a Florentine fireplace covered with Della Robbia cherubs, a full-length angel or two which he called his dancing girls, and with sighs of joy sank his stone-chilled feet deeply into hot water poured into a copper pot which his wife had bought from a peasant in the Abruzzo and which was someday going to be filled to abundance with bronze chrysanthemums in some white American home among the flaming autumn hills, but right now . . . she poured another boiling kettle in. "I wish to heaven you would find out definitely once and for all that of course she does have a lover. Or even two or three. Or decide that you want her yourself. Just tell me please, so I don't have to overhear it at the opera." "It's too hot," he protested for the third time. "You don't have to scald me. And anyway, I hope she does have somebody if he's the right sort. I just don't want her jumping out of a top window of the Colosseum, or off St. Peter's balcony or even her own terrace, for Christ's sake. You know about the suicide we had in Germany." "But why should she—?" "I don't know, I can't tell. It's just a feeling I have."

An old bathrobe he had bought in Missouri to take with him to Oxford where it had been his heart's comfort and one sure joy was hugged round his shoulders, and cupids, winged but bodiless, alternating with rich purple clusters of grapes and gently prancing unicorns, looked down upon him from the low, beamed Rinascimento ceiling, justly famed. Their palazzo was listed in guidebooks and it seemed a shame that they could never remember once having been warm in it. His wife was bundled up in sweaters and an old ski jacket; she even sometimes wore gloves indoors in the damper weather, and George himself was turning into an alcoholic just from trying to get enough whiskey in himself to keep out the vicious mists. A glass of bourbon sat beside him on the marble floor.

9

What George Hartwell now recognized that in those days he must have been fighting off was no more than what Martha herself had spent so long fighting off—that around one corner he was going to run headlong into Jim Wilbourne. He told himself he was afraid she had got mixed up with an Italian, though it might not in the long run perhaps mean very much—Italians generally left the American women they made love to, or so ran the prevailing superstition. The question of her divorce would have been in it from the first, thus practically guaranteeing she would get hurt. But then he worried too that it might be the English or the Americans, whom one counted on to really mean it, or so the legends went, and hence might get lulled into trusting too implicitly for anything. That might be more damaging in the long run.

"Who is it?" he came right out at lunch once and asked her. "Who is it, Martha?" But as he had not led up to this demand in any way, she assumed, quite naturally, that he was referring to somebody who had just passed their table and told him a name they both knew of a girl from Siena who used to work at the consulate but had had to return home to live with her aunt, but what was she now doing back in Rome. He said he didn't know.

The day was misty and the light blurred, lavender and close all day, dim as the smoke from the chestnut braziers, on the branched trees of the Villa Borghese where the gravel smashed damply under the thin soles of Roman shoes. The crowds flowed out, engulfing and persistent; a passing tram blocked out whatever one might have thought one saw. Hartwell gave up worrying; suicide seemed out—she looked invariably blooming. He had enough to bother him, what with new government directives which occasioned the reorganization of the entire staff (by a miracle he stabilized himself, Martha and one or two others he wanted to keep upon the shaky scaffolding until it quieted down—these earth tremors left everybody panting). Then there was the thing of the ambassador's getting poison off the ceiling paint—*Ceiling paint?* No Roman ever believed this, just as no American ever doubted it. Solemn assurances eventually were rendered by a U.S. medical staff that the thing had actually taken place. The Romans howled. You could judge how close you came to being permanent here by how much you doubted it.

Martha forgot to come one evening and help Grace Hartwell out with the Coggins', who had to be invited somewhere occasionally; they had to be acknowledged or clamours went up from their admirers. George made a monstrous effort and kept them out of the festival plans now being talked in reference to Spoleto where no one who remotely resembled them would be included, a thing they would never have understood. Martha rang up late, excusing herself on the grounds of some trouble with her maid. Maid trouble was always a standard excuse among Americans, and though it seemed almost Italian to lie to close friends, Grace Hartwell accepted it not to risk upsetting George.

"You abandoned me, just the same," she told Martha. "And that girl now is into some trouble over her work permit."

"She never had one at all," said Martha, who knew the straight of the story. "She agreed to help at the shop or be allowed to hang around just to learn Italian. She wanted experience instead of money."

"I don't know how much experience she got," said Grace, "or for that matter had already, but the proprietor had a fight with his relatives who are all out of work and say she's taking food out of their mouths and now she's been reported somewhere. The Coggins' seem to have got her out of it just by having so many friends at the Istituto Musicale di Roma, but now she's out of work."

"Unemployment is on the rise," said Martha flippantly, making Grace cross.

"There is so little for young people in Rome," said Grace, "they don't know what to do with her. It seems all the young Italians—"

"They can always send her back," said Martha.

But seeing that she had made Grace Hartwell angry, an almost impossible feat, she invited Grace and Dorothy Coggins to tea at Babbington's on the Piazza di Spagna. They were joined by Rita Wilbourne, who had been at Grace's. Dorothy Coggins said she used to come here often before Jean left the glove shop which was right across the street. Grace Hartwell gave full attention to Rita, who always looked tentative in Italy, rather like an ailing bird, but who, at least today, was subdued in what she wore, a navy dress and dark beret. Grace seemed to feel that given enough scones to eat she might actually be fixed in place in some way so far lacking. But Rita protested that she felt much better since some friends took her up to Switzerland, a civilized country.

Martha, who liked Grace and often used to confide in her, now felt herself so utterly bored she wondered if she could make it through to a second cup of tea, when suddenly, as if a signal had been given, they all found themselves deeply involved in talking about a new couple who had just come out from the States. They were soon examining these people in about every verbal way that exists, briskly, amiably, with enormous, almost profound curiosity, not at all unkindly, hoping for the best and not missing anything, from the two children's immediate cleverness with the language (they reminded Grace of *English* children. "Oh, yes, you're right," Martha enthusiastically agreed. "It's their *socks!*") to the woman's new U.S. clothes and probable family background, somewhat superior, they thought, to the husband's, who had worn a huge Western hat (he taught in Texas) down the Via Nazionale and was trailed around by knots of people, some of whom believed him to be a famous movie director. This was really rather funny, when one considered that he was actually an authority on Virgil, though Grace said she did not know which was funnier, to consider an authority on Virgil in a cowboy hat on the Via Nazionale, or in Texas in any sort of headgear, and Dorothy Coggins said that Texas was getting way way up, culturally speaking; that remark only proved what an ancient Roman Grace was getting to be. And Rita said that Jim loathed Italian hats and would not have one. Martha did not recall he ever had a hat at all.

"Richard doesn't mind anything Italian," said Dorothy. "He's simply gone on the place. Jean has a modelling job now," she told Martha. "I thought at first I'd have to arrange for her to go home; she was running around too much, meeting too many of these boys who just hang around places. I don't know what they do. I can never understand. Their families are well off, I suppose, but still I— You got it for her, didn't you, Martha?" "Why, no," said Martha, "I don't think so." "She mentioned you to that designer—what's her name?—Rossi. The little elegant one on the Via Boncompagni, and you were just the right one for her to know. She had to lose fifteen pounds—she ate nothing but salami for ten days. They were to call you up and she was sure—" "They didn't, but it's all right." "She thinks you got it for her." "Well, I—" Martha suddenly knew nothing to say. It looked clever of Jean to go to that one shop and mention her; but it had been perhaps merely luck. It was the sort of haphazard luck the girl had. "She admires you so," said Dorothy Coggins, with housewifely openness. "She always did. It really is amazing," she added. "I can't see anything amazing about it," said Grace, with her generous laugh. They had all paused and were looking, with more admiration than not, at Martha, and Rita said, "What a lovely pin—I must borrow it sometime to copy it." It was something she had had forever. She felt silent and alone in a certain shared secrecy with the pin—its quiet upcurving taste enclosing amethysts—and though she said she would lend it to Rita sometime she had no intention of doing so.

The women sat together, in their best suits and hats, shoes damp from the streets, handbags beside them, at a corner table while the early dusk came on and the soupy traffic thickened outside. The ceiling was low, dark and beamed in the English manner; the place a favorite haunt of the quieter English colony. The Brownings might have just gone out. Yet under the distant assurance of even that name lurked some grisly Renaissance tale. Martha found her gloves and asked for the check.

Afterwards, she drove with Grace to carry Dorothy

Coggins up the Gianicolo to the American Academy to meet her husband. They left Rita to catch a cab home. "It will be a blessing," said Dorothy as Grace fended through traffic, "if she has another baby as soon as she can; she's not going to be happy until she does. I know that from my own experience."

"Well, if she could just—" Grace Hartwell broke off, fighting traffic for dear life. She and Martha were quite solidified in not wanting to hear just what Dorothy's experience had been.

When she dropped Dorothy off, she drove around for a time among the quiet streets above the city, also above the weather, for up here it seemed clear and cold and glimpses of the city showed below them framed in a long reach of purple cloud.

"You didn't mind my bringing Rita?" she asked Martha.

"No," said Martha, and then she said, "I see a lot of Jim, you know."

"I thought something like that, this afternoon, I don't know why. I really cannot think why. I think it was when she asked you for that pin. Isn't that amazing? Well, I won't tell George."

"I know you won't," said Martha.

"I just hate seeing nice people get hurt," said Grace,

somewhat shyly. She and George had fallen in love at a college dance. They had never, they did not need to tell you, loved anybody else but one another.

"I don't know who is supposed to be nice people," said Martha, with a little laugh.

Grace did not answer and Martha added, "I don't want, I honestly do not want to embarrass George in any way."

"Why, it's possible he won't ever hear about it at all. Unless everybody does. Or unless the marriage breaks up or something. Is that what you want to happen?"

Martha fell completely silent. This was the trouble with the run of women, considered as a tribe, with their husbands—George, Jim, and Richard—to talk about and other families to analyze. How they assembled all those alert, kind-tongued comparisons! How instantly they got through an enormous pot of tea and a platter of pastries! How they went right straight to the point, or what they considered to be the only point possible. To Martha it was not the point at all. The fact of her trusting Grace was the more remarkable in that she understood, even in advance, that they would from now on in some way be foreign to one another.

"I don't know that I want anything to happen," said Martha.

"Rita came over," said Grace, "to talk about—"

"Oh do stop it," said Martha, laughing, but somewhat put out as well. "You're trying to say it wasn't about me."

"You know, I honestly feel tired of it already," Grace said. She paused. "I'll think of it all as we were, as you and George and I always have been, all these years. I'm going to do that," she reiterated, and began to accelerate. Pulling her chin up sharply, a habit for preserving her chin line, and gripping the wheel with hands in worn pigskin gloves, she went swinging and swirling down the Gianicolo, past the high balustraded walls of those tall terra-cotta villas. She remained firm and skillful—a safe driver—her reddish-brown hair, streaked with grey, drawn up rather too tall from her wide freckled brow so forthrightly furrowed (like many people with warm, expressive faces, the thin skin texture of nice women, she was prematurely lined). But now, Martha noticed, her face looked strained as well.

"Confidences are a burden, I know," said Martha. "I'm sorry, Grace."

"It isn't keeping secrets I mind. You know that. No, it isn't that at all."

Martha did not ask her to define things further, for to encounter love of the innocent, protective sort which

George and Grace Hartwell offered her and which she had in the past found so necessary and comforting seemed to her now somewhat like a risk, certainly an embarrassment, almost a sort of doom. Grace did not press any further observations upon her, did not kiss her when she was ready to get out of the car. She waved and smiled—there was something touching about it, a sort of gallantry, and Martha was sensitive to the exaggeration, the hint of selfishness, which this reaction contained. She did not blame Grace, but she read her accurately. She was protective of her husband, the sensitive area was here, and here also was written plainly that Martha was more of a help to George Hartwell than she herself had known. Somehow she thinks now I'm in bad faith and she in good, Martha saw. Does she think I can live for George Hartwell?

She took off her damp topcoat and the hat with which she had honored the tea and saw on the telephone pad a note saying that Signor Wilbourne had called.

10

"Martha?"

Whether at home or in the office, at whatever time of day, the name, her own, coming at her with the curious, semi-hoarse catch in it, seemed to fall through her hearing and onward, entering deep spaces within her. She listened as though she had never heard it before, and almost at times forgot to answer. Hurried, he was generally going on anyway to what he meant to tell her, the clatter of some bar in the background, he would be shifting whatever clutch of books or brief-case he had with him to unfold a scrap of paper and read an address. Then she would write it down. There were streets she'd never heard of, areas she did not know existed, bare-swept rooms at the tops of narrow stairs, the murmur of apartment life from some other floor or some distance back of this one, the sounds of the street. The wires of small electric stoves glowed across the dim twilights of these rooms, and if she reached them first, she would sit quietly waiting for him to come, drawing the heater close to warm her damp feet, wearing one of the plain tweed suits she wore to work, her scarf and coat hung up, her face bent seriously forward. She thought of nothing, nothing at all.

She would hear his footsteps on the stair striking, as his voice on the phone did, directly against her hearing, but when the door opened she would scarcely look up, if at all, and he on his part gave her scarcely more than a passing glance, turning almost at once to put his coat up. Yet the confrontation, as brief as that, was absolute and profound. It was far more ancient than Rome.

"Is it okay here? Is it all right?" To a listener, he might have been a landlord speaking. She sat with her hands quietly placed beside her. "It's like the others. There's nothing to say about it, is there?" "Well, it's never warm enough. Someday we'll . . ." "Do what?" "I don't know. Go right into the Excelsior, I guess. Say to hell with it." "But I like it here." "You're a romana."

His cheek, the high bone that crossed in a straight,

horizontal line, pressed coldly against her own; it was damp from the outside air. His hands warmed momentarily beneath her jacket. His quick remarks, murmured at her, blurred off into her hearing—stones thrown in the sea. In the long upswing of her breath she forgot to answer, and tumbled back easily with him against the bed's length. "God, there's never enough time!" "Forget it." "Yes . . . I will . . . yes. . . ."

In these beginnings, she often marvelled to know if she was being made love to or softly mauled by a panther, and that marvelling itself could dwindle, vanishing into the twin bars of the electric fire, or the flicker of a white shirt upon a chair. She could reach the point of wondering at nothing.

Yet something—some word from without them both did come to her—either then or in recollection of those little widely spaced-out little rooms hidden among the crooked roofs of Rome, where the mists curled by, and thought stood still and useless, desiccated, crumbling, and perishing; it was only a phrase: Run slowly, slowly, horses of the night. It fell through her consciousness as her own name had done, catching fire, mounting to incandescence, vanishing in a slow vast cloudy image silently among the grey skies.

Sometimes he gave her coarse Italian brandy to drink out of a bottle he might have found time to stop in a bar and buy; and she sometimes had thought of stuffing bread and cheese in her bag, but they were mainly almost without civility—there was never any glass for the brandy or any knife for the cheese, and if anyone had hung a picture or brought in a flower or two their consciousness of one another might have received, if not a killing blow, at least a heavy abrasion.

She asked him once why he did not simply come to her, but there was something about Rome he instinctively knew from the start and chose to sidestep. Ravenous for gossip, the Romans looked for it in certain chosen hunting fields—nothing would induce them to rummage around in the poorer quarters of Trastevere or wonder what went on out near San Lorenzo. And anyway—

And anyway, she understood. It was merely a question, perhaps, of furniture. The time or two he did stop by her place, ringing her up from a tobacco shop or restaurant nearby, they almost always disagreed about something. Disagreed was not quite the word; it was a surprise to her that she still found him, after everything that went on, somewhat difficult to talk to. She remembered the times in Venice and later in Rome that she had sparred with him, fighting at something intractable in his nature, and the thought of getting into that sort of thing any more made her draw back.

She just didn't want to. Perhaps it was a surprise to him that she never asked him anything any more; she never tried to track him down. Did he miss that or didn't he? Did he ask himself? And if he had would he have known what to answer? He was busy—that was one thing, of course. Committees had been set up—there was a certain modest stir about economic planning on certain American lines proceeding at a level far below the top governmental rank, only in educational circles, but still— He thought of plunging off into field work, studying possibilities of industry in the south of Italy. "Then you might never come back," said Martha. "You mean to Rome?" "Oh, no, I meant—it's a separate world." She did not think he would ever do it. "You don't think I'll ever do it, do you?" She seemed even to herself to have drifted away for a time, and finally murmured or thought she had said, "I don't know." She was tired herself, with mimeograph ink on her hands and a whole new library list to set up, and her brain gone numb at so much bandying about of phrases like "the American image abroad." "What did you say?" he asked her. "I said I don't know." She rallied. "It's a worthwhile project, certainly." "Thank you, Mrs. Ingram." His tone stung her; she glanced up and tears came to her eyes. "I'm sorry," he said, with a certain stubborn slant on the words.

He had been leaning against her mantelpiece talking down to where she sat in the depths of a wing chair, sometimes toying with objects—small statuary, glass clusters and paperweights—distributed on the marble surface. When he pulled her up against him by way of breaking off a conversation that had come to nothing, his elbow struck a china image to the floor. The apartment was rented furnished, only half such things were hers and this was not. He helped her clean the fragments and must have said a dozen times how much he regretted it, asking too, "What was it?" "A little saint, or maybe goddess . . . I don't know." "If you don't know, then maybe it wasn't so good, after all." She smiled at the compliment. "I wish we were back in some starved little room," she said, "where nothing can get broken." "So do I," he agreed and left soon after.

Reflecting, she was not long in coming upon the truth the little rooms made plain: that they had struck a bargain that lay deeply below the level of ordinary speech; in fact, that in rising toward realization in the world where things were said, it only ran terrible risks of crippling and loss.

And yet one afternoon when the rain stopped and there was even a red streak of late sun in the clear simple street below, she felt gentle and happy and asked him to walk down in the street for just a little way. And then when he consented a dog trotted up and put its nose in her palm; it would have laid all of life at her feet like a bone. A cat purred near the open furnace of a pizzeria, which burned like a deep-set eye of fire in the stony non-colour of a winter day, and a child ran out with bare arms into the cold, its mother following after, shouting "Pino! Pino!" and holding up a little coat. When they left the pizzeria, he lit a cigarette leaning against a damp wall and said, All right, all right, if she wanted to they would go away for the weekend somewhere. She looked up startled and gratified, as though at an unexpected gift. It had been somewhat offhandedly thrust at her and yet its true substance was with it.

II

They drove to the sea in what started out to be fine weather but thickened over damply. Nevertheless, he had been full of a run of recklessly funny talk and stories ever since he got off the tram and crossed the sunlit street to meet her, way out near the Laterano, and the mood persisted. The feeling between them was, though nobody had mentioned it, that they would never be back at all. They took turns driving.

Martha admired the artichoke fields warm in the new sun and recalled a peasant who had ploughed up a whole Aphrodite in his field and didn't know what to do with her, for if he told anybody his little farm would be made an archeological area; he wouldn't get to raise any more artichokes for a decade or two. So he and his family kept hiding the statue and every now and then someone would be smuggled in to have a go at wondering how much could be got for her in devious ways and the whole thing went on for a year or so, but in the end the farmer buried her again and let her rest in peace; he could never decide whom he could trust, for everybody had a different theory, told a different story, and offered him a different sum. He then went back to raising artichokes. "So every field I see I think of Aphrodite under it," said Martha. This was not true, but she did think of it now—the small compact mindless lovely head, the blank blind exalted eyes, deep in the dark earth. "Imagine finding Aphrodite and not knowing what to do with her," he said. He began to cough.

The racking of this particular cough had gone on for weeks now. He said he would never understand Martha for never being sick. The Wilbournes were always in the thick of illnesses; there had not only been Rita's miscarriage, which had afflicted him with a tenacious sort of despair, a sense of waste and reasonlessness, the worse for being almost totally abstract. What kind of home could be had in this city, in this entire country? (Here the sun, distinctly weakening, had about faded out; he seemed to be grasping for it.) The Italians didn't even have a word for home. Casa. It was where you hung your hat, and slept, and froze, and tried to keep from dying. Oh, Lord, thought Martha, getting weary of him. To her, Rome was a magnificent city in any weather and she moved in it easily with friends in four languages at least—she had not been Gordon Ingram's student for nothing. The city's elegant, bitter surfaces were hers naturally, as a result of his taste and judgment; and there were people about who knew this, in their own way of knowing, from the instant she stepped across the threshold of a salotto. She had luck, as well. She rented from a contessa in Padova, who counted her a friend; if she told all this to Jim Wilbourne he would class her with the Coggins' who had got invited to a vendemmia in Frascati a short time after they arrived.

At the sea they sat before a rough fire in the albergo (there were no other guests) and her mind wheeled slowly round him like a gull. It was going to dawn on him someday, she thought, how well she got along, how easily she got things, not the sort of things the Coggins' got which nobody wanted, but the sort of things one coveted. She started out of this, startling herself; this was wrong, all wrong—he was better than that. He was self-amused, even in his furies, and never lost the thread of reason (this being one reason Italians preyed on him; the reason in a reasonless quarrel delighted them, they would probably have gone on fighting with him for a generation or so, if he had remained, for when the maid stole the case of economics texts on loan from the States and was forced to admit it, she returned to him books in the same case, weighed within an etto of the original weight, the books even being in English and some, she pointed out, having been printed in the States: they were mainly mystery novels, but included a leather-bound history of World War I dedicated to the Veterans of Foreign Wars—he found this appropriate). And even he would admit that what he needed most for his nerves in a country so uncivilized was an evening at the bowling alley, a stroll through a drugstore, a ride down the turnpike, an evening at the neighborhood movie house. These things were not as much a myth to Martha as might be thought to look at her, in her classic Roman greys and black, for Woolworth's and Radio City had once stabilized her more than human voices. He believed this, and the rain sprang up off the sea, lashing in ropes against the tall windows. Her heart sank. "It's so nice here in summer," she said faintly. His face had turned silent; in Italy he had acquired a touch of despair that she felt sorry for. He could make her feel responsible for the weather.

She never knew if he heard her at all. A shift of wind off the sea had blown one of the glass doors wide, and a maid rushed through to close it, but they scarcely noticed, if at all. They had reached the shore, an extremity of sorts, and had already discovered themselves on the other side of a wall, shut, enclosed, in the garden that everyone knows is there, where even the flowers are carnivorous and stir to avid life at the first footfall. He had caught her hand, near the cup, among the silver. She sat with her face half-turned aside, until her hand and arm reddened from the fire. She did not remember leaving the table and going upstairs.

The room where they stood for a time, clinging together a step from the closed door, was unlighted, dark, though on this troubled coast it seemed a darkness prepared and waiting with something like self-knowledge, to be discovered, mapped, explored, claimed, possessed, and changed for good, no inch of it left innocent of them, nothing she had ever felt to be alive not met and dealt with. They were radical and unhurried as if under imperial orders, and it seemed no one night could contain them; yet it managed to. As she fell asleep she heard the rain stop; it had outdistanced them by a little, as though some sort of race had been going quietly on.

The next morning there was a thin light on the sea which hung leaden and waveless below their windows, its breast burnishing slightly, convexly meeting the fall of the light, like a shield. She saw a bird on the window-sill outside. Its feathers blew, ruffling in the wind, and once it shifted and looked in for a moment; she saw the tiny darting gleam of its regard.

The silver light held through the whole day. They drove far up the coast toward Pisa and she feared for a moment toward midday, voicelessly without decision as they seemed to be, they would come full circle at Genoa, where she had first seen him, in which case the sky would fall in broken masses of grey light. But the way is longer than it might be thought to be, and the slowly unwinding journey seemed perpetual, the fields and villages strict and sharply drawn with winter, the coast precipitous and wild, vanishing only to reappear; and their own speed on nearly deserted roads was deceptive—no matter what the speedometer said, they seemed adrift. They came on a fishing village and stayed there; she could never remember the name of it, but perhaps she never knew.

Where they were drifting, however, was not toward Genoa and the sky falling, nor to any mythical kingdom, but like thousands of others before and after them, it was only toward Sunday afternoon. He was sitting putting on his shoe in the pensione when the shoelace suddenly snapped in his narrow fingers, jarring him into a tension that had seemed to be gone forever; if there was anything he immediately returned himself to, after the ravishment of strange compelling voyages, it was order; he was wrenched by broken shoelaces, and it was to that slight thing she traced what he said when they were leaving: "It disturbs me to think I'm the one you aren't going to forget—yet it's true, I know it is."

His arms were around her; he was human and gentle; but she filled up instantly with panic—it was time he had let in on them, in one phrase. Had he meant to be so drastic as that? But it had always been there, she reasoned desperately, and though watching the abyss open without alarm is always something of a strain, she tried to manage it. Yet going down the stair she felt numb and scraped her wrist against a rough wall surface. Reaching the car ahead of him, she sat, looking at the surface of the harshly rubbed skin, which had shaved up in places like thinly rolled trimming of chalk, and the flecking of red beneath, the wonder of having blood at all at a moment when her ample, somewhat slow, slightly baroque body had just come to rest as finally as stone.

Miles later on the way back to Rome she asked him, "What about you? Are you going to forget it?" He glanced at her at once. "No." And repeated it: "No."

On that she would be able to stay permanently, she believed; it was her raft on the long, always outflowing tide of things, and once back in Rome could linger, not being obliged to be anywhere, in the bare strict narrow rented room, and ride the wake of his footsteps hurrying down toward the empty street, but one day she discovered on walking home alone that the rain had stopped for once, and travelling a broad street—Via Cola di Rienzo—that rose toward a high bridge above the Tiber, the sky grew grey and broad and flashed with light into which the tramontana came bitterly streaming, drawing even the wettest and deadest leaves up into it, and the whole yawning city beneath was resonant with air like wind entering an enormous bell. This is the center of the world, she thought, this city, with a certain pride, almost like a native might, or should have.

And passing through the post office, far across the gigantic enclosed hall of a thousand rendezvous, and small disbursements for postal money orders and electric bills and letters sent pòsta aerea to catch the urgent plane and the smell of ink and blotted bureaucratic forms and contraband cigarettes, she saw Gordon Ingram leaning on a heavy mahogany cane, the sort of thing he would either bring to Europe with him or find for himself the instant he arrived. His back was toward her, that heavy-shouldered bulk, and he was leaning down to write on a sheet of paper, but even while she watched, something must have gone wrong with the pen for he shook it twice, then threw it aside and walked away. The letter fluttered to the ground and she soon went there and picked it up but by that time a heel or two had marked it in walking past.

Yet she made out clearly, in handsome script, the best Italian: "Sebbene (whereas) . . . tu m'abbia accusato di ció che ti piace chiamare inumanitá (you have accused me of what it gives you satisfaction to call inhumanity, you must realize if you have any mentality at all, that this man in spite of his youth and attractiveness is far less human than anyone of my generation could possibly be, without the least doubt. He takes an interest in you because he must live in this way to know that he is alive at all, and his behavior is certain to disappoint a woman like yourself, such as I have taught you to be, in such a manner as to make you wish that it could never be said by anyone including yourself that you were ever in any contact with him. You know that whatever else you may say or think, I have never lied to you—this you cannot deny—I have never once lied to you, whereas you have done nothing but pride yourself on your continual lying as though it were some sort of accomplishment, an art you had mastered so well you could use it carelessly [pensarci])—"

She went home holding the letter in one hand and reached the apartment with the heel of one shoe in the other, limping, because she had twisted the heel off in the irregular paving of the piazzetta below. She had spent the morning helping George Hartwell draw up a new lecture program, and there had been the interview with the priest who wanted to start a liberal newspaper in a small town near Bari. At last anyway, she had a letter, a direct word. She hung up her umbrella, coat and scarf, but dripped still, a limping trail into the big salotto, which, awaiting her in the quiet, looked utterly vacant, as disinhabited as if it were rented out afresh every three months, and she thought, He can't have written this; he is dead. Nobody is ever coming here again.

She fell face downward on the couch and slept, half-recalling and half-dreaming—which, she did not know, and why, she did not know, though the whole held no horror for her whatsoever any more than some familiar common object might—the story of a man who shot and wounded a she-wolf on his way home through the woods at twilight, and coming home, found his wife dead on the couch, a trail of blood leading inward from the door. She was awakened by a banging shutter.

She went out to the terrace and saw that the clouds had cleared before the wind and were racing in long streamers like swift ships, and that a moon, so deeply cold it would always do to think of whenever cold was mentioned, raced without motion. The city beneath it lay like a waste, mysterious, empty discovery, cold and vaulted beneath it, channelling the wind. It came to her for the first time to wonder, standing out on her empty, winter-disarrayed terrace, if a cold like that might not be life's truest definition, since there was so much of it.

And certain cold images of herself were breaking in upon her now, as though she had waked up in a thunder-ridden night and had seen an image of herself in the mirror, an image that in the jagged and sudden flash seemed to leap unnaturally close. What am I doing? Am I asleep sitting straight up? A thousand times she had said to life in the person of a bird, brilliant and wise in the cage of a friend, or a passing dog (just as she had said to Gordon Ingram), I forgive you everything, please forgive me too, but getting no answer from either, her mind went on discriminating. She had not been Gordon Ingram's student for nothing and she longed to discuss it with him:

If life unreels from an original intuition, what if that intuition was only accident, what if it was impulse, a blind leap in the dark? An accident must be capable of being either a mistake or a stroke of luck, depending on what it is in relation to whom it happens to. So what do you think of this one, since you were the victim of it? Before you are quite gone, forever and ever, answer that for me at least.

But he was silent; Gordon Ingram was always silent.

Jim Wilbourne, however, told her many things about himself and (she had not been Gordon Ingram's student for nothing) none of them were supremely interesting things; she listened but was not utterly arrested, sometimes she half-listened. So he said, "Listen, Martha—listen," and she did stop the car (it being her turn to drive) coming back from the sea in the wet sea-heavy night, and she did try to listen, but traffic sprang up from everywhere—there was a confluence of roads and they all led to Rome, a glare and snarl and recklessness in the rain and dark, and someone shouted, "Stupida! Ma guarda! Guarda!" They poured past her like the hastening streams of the damned. She turned her face to him and he was talking, haltingly; he fell almost at once into platitudes and she wondered that the person whose face she encountered in the depths of her dreams had nothing more remarkable to say than this.

It did not escape him. He wanted to return everything to its original clear potential, to say that love, like life, is not remarkable, it is as common as bread; but every contact between the two of them was not common; it was remarkable; he was stopped before he started. "I'm listening; I'm listening," she said.

"It's the way you're listening."

"Don't let that matter to you," she said gently, kindly,

for the shadow of some nature far beyond anything that had happened to her occasionally came to her. "I live in a mirror, at the bottom of a mirror somewhere."

"I think we both do; it's why we make love so well."

"There must be some way to stop it . . . to go back to where we might have been, to change. I always wanted to think of it differently. You remember I told you—"

"Yes, I remember." He urged her to drive on; the stop was dangerous, and presently said out of a long sequence of thought not told to her: "I simply can't ever believe there's any way back from anything." The force of the statement reached her, and she sensed it as distantly related to fury. He had made another jump, she realized, and now there was no turning back from that either. She had finally, like any other woman, to hold on the best way she could.

part four

12

Coming up from the winter's recollections was what she and George Hartwell had to do every so often, to keep from drowning.

They were still on the terrace, and it was still Sunday morning, a healing timelessness of sun, though Hartwell went on gnawing at things he drew up out of fathomless reservoirs.

"And did you know," he was saying, "and did you fully realize, that Wilbourne got me to recommend him for an Italian government grant? He was going to study the economic picture south of Naples—the self-sacrificing servant of his times, he was harkening to duty's voice, he was going to leave the world a better place. Then what did he do but turn around and use that very grant as a lever to land his fat job back in the States."

"I'm not surprised," said Martha.

"But think what a hell of a position it put me in," Hartwell complained.

"Well, why did you let him talk you into it?"

"I thought you wanted him here. I thought you—"

"You thought *I* did it?"

"Something like that."

"It wasn't my idea," she said. "It was only that he did talk about it. I suppose, for a time, he considered staying on; he may even have believed that he meant to."

"But you said you weren't surprised."

"I wasn't . . . no . . . when he changed his mind, you mean? No, I wasn't too surprised. He only existed in relation to Gordon." There had always been the three of them, she thought; they had got stuck in the same frame forever.

"You mean destructively, of course," George Hartwell grumbled. He wondered what portion of the service they had reached in Mass, for though not a Catholic, he could hope that it was some deep and serious portion which could bite him up whole and take elaborate care to lift him back out of this pit he had blundered into on a fine Sunday morning.

"Did you see a little white-haired American lady on your way in?" Martha asked. "She was wearing a blue feather hat with a close veil over her hair and face, and a matching blue coat. She was bowlegged."

"Martha," said Hartwell, "aren't you going to spare me anything?"

He had begun to laugh. The whole thing was crazy, and probably had been all along. There wasn't any little old lady in blue. That was one certain fact. It was something to tie to. It enabled him to keep on laughing.

But there had been no laughter for him at all from any source on that February day back in the winter when the phone rang in his office and the voice said:

"This is Gordon Ingram, Mr. Hartwell; may I see you for a short time?"

"Where are you? Where are you?" was all he could think of to say; that and "Yes, Albergo Nazionale . . . of course, right away."

To his amazement a chill like a streak of ice had run down his spine; he went out in no time, breaking three appointments, grabbing a cab rather than take the car. Had the man already called his wife? Did she know? If so, she was likely driving blindly away somewhere, fodder for the next highway crash, or more deliberately, walking straight off into the Tiber would do just as well.

He felt himself in the grip of fates and furies. In the dank, gusty February day, every step seemed bringing him nearer to the moment when statues speak and old loves appear.

Albergo Nazionale ran inward from a discreet doorway. The rugs were heavy and the décor firm. He searched among the sofas, the coffee tables, the écritoires, the alcoves, and bronze gods taming horses, for a shape ponderous and vast, a heavy thigh and a foot like an elephant's, and toward the last he was spinning like a top and had whirled upon the desk clerk, saying, "I'm looking for a Signor Ingram, un professore americano." But before he could get that out altogether, a hand touched his sleeve, and it was only Robert Inman, English and slight with sandy hair severely thinned, a classmate at Balliol. "I say, George, I've tried this makes three times to stop you, can't have changed so much as all that, you know." It could not have been Robert Inman who had telephoned, yet it had been. There was no Ingram on the register.

George Hartwell lived through a weak scotch in an armchair which threatened to swallow him whole, so small was he already in addition to feeling unreal, extended a dinner invitation, reviewed old histories, and afterwards, still in bleary weather, he walked up to the Campidoglio and stood looking through a heavy iron grill at something he had remembered wondering at before, back in his early days in Rome, the enormous hand from the statue of an emperor, standing among other shards in the barred recess. It was the dumbness of the detached gesture, there forever, suggesting not so much the body it was broken from as the sky it was lifted toward—one could be certain all through the centuries of similar skies. And with very little trouble he could find which step Gibbon was probably sitting on when he thought of *Decline and Fall*, but why do it unless perhaps he wanted to plant him down on the cold stone and catch pneumonia? And what indeed did he have to think of that was a match for Gibbon? He had to realize that in missing three appointments at least—two of which had to do with Italian cultural organizations interested in cooperating with American exchange programs—he had not done a good thing and that now he would have to dictate letters explaining that his son was in an accident and that he had thought for a time of flying home. Anyway, it was too late now.

He walked a bit and in passing near the post office saw the Wilbourne car, which was now fairly well known in Rome because so much had got stolen off it at one time or another, and certain quarrels had centered about it as it had once been jointly owned with another couple who complained that the Wilbournes (though the car was in their possession each time it was rifled) insisted that the expense of each misfortune be shared and shared alike. The body was a sort of dirty cream which Hartwell did not like, possibly because he did not like the Wilbournes, so why be called upon to stop and wait and why, when Jim Wilbourne appeared alone, ask him into the German beer hall nearby to share a stein and bend his ear about this odd thing—this misunderstood telephone call—as if by talking about it, it would be just odd and nothing more. And it seemed, too that only by talking could he say that from the first he had felt a concern for Martha, that she had stirred his sympathies from the first and he had learned her story a little at a time. This, too, he judged, was only a way of talking about people for once, instead of programs, programs—one built up a kind of ravenous appetite for individuals, for the old-time town life he, back in Missouri, had had once and called the past. He was winding up by saying, "Of course, don't repeat any of this to Martha," and there was a certain kind of pause hanging in the air and Jim Wilbourne carefully lit a cigarette behind his hands, worrying the match five or six times before it went out, and Hartwell thought, Oh God, Oh my God, having caught it on one side now I'm catching it on the other. I didn't know and yet I must have known.

He also thought: She is not this important to me, for all this about her to happen in one afternoon.

The trouble was she was neurotic. He had got dragged into her exile's paranoia as into a whirlpool. He foresaw the time when the only individuals would be neurotics. They were the only people who still had the nerve to demand an answer. He doubted if Jim Wilbourne was neurotic or that he would qualify as an individual, but he without a doubt had a sort of nerve balance that so obviously related him to women it seemed in the most general sense to be a sort of specific of blessing, like rain or sun, and why shouldn't she, in common with everybody else, have sun and rain? Who was to rule her out of golden shores? But with her there would always be more to it than that. Hartwell had blundered into this picture and now he wanted out.

"Did you ever know this guy?" Jim Wilbourne asked.

"Who, her husband? Well, only by reputation. He was at one time a leading American philosopher, or that was the direction he took early on. There were a couple of books . . . some theories of goodness, relating action to idealism . . . something like that. I remember one of them excited me. I read half of it standing in the college library one afternoon. . . ." One long-ago fall afternoon at Harvard. What reaches out of nowhere to touch and claim us? At a certain age, on a certain sort of afternoon, it may be any book we pick out from a shelf. "But perhaps you've read it too."

"Oh, Lord, no. I read practically nothing out of my field. I know that's not a good thing. It makes me laugh to think—I'd laid all sort of plans for doing some catching up on reading in Italy, after I learned the language, of course." He ended by coughing badly.

"You have learned it," Hartwell said, complimenting effort. "Damned near killed me. It was a hell of a lot of work."

"You're telling me." Hartwell gulped his way into a second beer.

At the end of the encounter, catching a cab back to the office, refusing a ride, Hartwell felt outdone and silly. He envied Jim Wilbourne his cool intelligence, his quick judgments, his refusal to drink too much. I am the world's most useless citizen, he thought, an impractical cultural product, a detached hand reaching out, certainly changing nothing, not even touching anything. I am the emperor of Rome—I shall be stabbed in a corridor.

He longed for his own warm table and his wife's brown eyes, under whose regard he had so often reassembled his soul.

13

"*There was* always something rather depressing to me," said Hartwell with a laugh, "about all those damn ceramics. She kept on turning them out as if her life depended on it, and every one of them was in the worst possible taste."

"She knew the market back in the States," Martha said kindly. "I think that's what she had in mind."

"It's no wonder the Italians preyed on them. There was something about some chickens."

"The landlord's cousins kept some chickens out on the terrace next door, which was disturbing," Martha related, "and then when the Wilbournes got an order through the condominio to remove the chickens, they put some ducks there instead. The Wilbournes killed and ate the ducks. That was not as bad, however, as the fight over the electric bill."

"Oh, Lord," said Hartwell. "Even we had one of those. Martha, you never had a fight with Italians in your life."

"Never," said Martha, "but then I never tried setting up a business."

"I'm frankly glad as hell they're gone," said Hartwell. "If she started a business," he went on, unwisely, "it was probably out of desperation. She never seemed very well. If a vote of sympathy was taken, she'd get mine."

They had taken Rita Wilbourne for a drive one day to Tivoli—he and his wife—and had discovered near there in the low mountains a meadow full of flowers. It was as near a miracle as they could have hoped for, for it was misty when they left Rome and raining when they returned, but here she grew excited and jumped out of the car and walked out into the sun. Hartwell and his wife Grace sat in the car and spoke of her; she was unhappy, displaced in life, and alone far too much.

She had walked on away from them, here and there, in a brightly striped raincoat, always with her back to them, so that it was easy to imagine she might be crying. She talked about too many different things. Grace Hartwell worried about her. "Men like Jim Wilbourne are difficult," she said. "They're bitter, for one thing.

I dislike bitter men—they are nothing but a drain." Yet when Rita came back to the car she had not been crying at all that Hartwell could see. She had found some bits of mosaic to copy in the bramble-covered remains of something—a villa, a bath, a tower—a whole acanthus leaf done in marble; her eyes were flat, bright, almost black; she was like a wound-up doll. She said it was marvellous to see the sun; she said it was wonderful to find a meadow full of flowers; she said it was quite unusual to find a whole acanthus leaf in marble. Who was she to demand George Hartwell's fealty? She was an American girl who happened to be walking across a meadow near Tivoli; she thought automatically of what she could do with what she found there. Martha Ingram hardly heard him when he spoke of sympathizing with her; she correctly judged that he was attacking Jim Wilbourne.

"What have you got against Jim? I doubt his being so bad as you think. There was nothing whatever bad about him, in an extraordinary sense."

"Yes," said Hartwell, "but who do you think is? Always excepting Gordon Ingram, of course?"

She fell silent; he wondered if he had got to her. Self-appointed and meddlesome, she could certainly call him, but he would stop her if it killed him, he thought, and it probably would. It was then she flashed at him with sudden definition, like an explosion of tinder:

"But I love them both. Haven't you understood that was the reason for it all?"

And the one to be stopped was himself.

He sat and mopped his brow as though in a period of truce, by himself, at least, much needed.

So they finally turned to business, having worn each other out.

The papers came out of her desk and he was leaning close to the shadow of the terrace wall to glance at some notes she could and did explain from memory—one thing clearly emerging from all this, like a negative from a slow developer, was how excellent she was; she seemed to have got up one morning and put her work on like a new dress. People were always calling George Hartwell up to tell him in assorted languages how lucky he was to have her, how lucky the United States of America was to have her, and in truth he himself had to marvel at how intelligently she could appear at varied distances in the conversation of salotti, terrazzi, giardini. He thought she would grow the torch of liberty out of her hand any day now, or at least show up photographed in some sleek expensive magazine, a model of the career woman abroad. She might even eclipse him: had he thought of that? He thought of it now, and decided that it did not supremely matter. In view of his long ambitious years, what a surprising thing, right now, to learn this about himself. Grace in leaving had been brimful of talk about their son, graduating at home, the solemn black mortarboard procession stretching and contracting, winding beneath green elms, every sun splotch another sort of hope and promise; the twin tears in Grace's eyes meant grandchildren beyond a doubt. Even when packing to leave, her son's future was infinitely exploding within her. She at some unknown hour had acquiesced to something: the shift in women's ambitions —true augur of the world. It was known to all, George realized, how much he drank, and Martha now was fetching him another, moving in and out among the azaleas. The truth at last emerges (he took the glass); but it had been there, relentlessly forming all this while.

"But what if the poor old bastard wants you, needs you? What if he dies?"

"I've been there already," she said, remembering how they had got the land away from her where it had all happened, she had signed the papers at Colonna's on the Piazza del Popolo and heard how the gun's roar faded along with the crash of the leaves.

"That isn't good enough!" said Hartwell, but her grey regard upon him was simply accidental, like meeting the eyes in a painting.

So there was no way around her.

I'll go myself, thought Hartwell, halfway down the scotch. In the name of humanity somebody had to, and it seemed, for one sustained, sustaining moment, that he actually would. He would go out of the apartment, reach his car, drive to the nearest telephone, call the airport for space on the first plane to New York. He could smell the seared asphalt of a New York summer, could see soot lingering on windowsills in the coarse sunlight, feel the lean of the cab turning into the hospital drive, every building in an island aspect, turning freely. An afternoon of dying. . . . A strange face in the door's dwindling square, rising above the muted murmur of a hospital at twilight: "I have come from your wife. You must understand she would come if she could, but she cannot. You must understand that she loves you, she said so: I heard her say so. She has been unavoidably detained . . . restrained? . . . stained? . . . mained?"

Then he knew it was time to go. He picked up all the documents, and put the last swallow down. The stairs were below. "Lunch with me this week." "Poor George, I think I upset you."

Poor George (he kept hearing it). Poor George, poor George, poor George. . . .

part

five

14

But she had never said Poor Jim, though he too had gone down that very stairway as shaken as he had ever been in his life or ever would be. Their parting had torn at him desperately—she saw it; it was visible. And all this on the first day of sun.

"Love . . . love . . . love . . ." The word kept striking over and again like some gigantic showpiece of a clock promptly, voraciously at work to mark midnight, though actually it was noon. Returning to her was what he kept talking about. "Yes, yes, I'll always be here," she replied.

But his total motion once begun carried him rapidly down and away, cortile and fountain, stairway and hidden turning—the illusion was dropping off like a play he had been in, when, at the last flight's turning, he came to an abrupt halt and stood confronting someone who had just come through the open portone and was now looking about for mailboxes or buzzers, a fresh-faced young man whose clear candid eyes had not yet known what stamped a line between the brows.

He was wearing a tropical-weight suit which would have been too optimistic yesterday, but was exactly right today. Second year university, just arrived this morning, Jim Wilbourne thought, holding to the bannister. The young man seemed to have brought the sun. Jim Wilbourne, fresh air from the portone fanning his winter-pale cheek, thought for the first time in months of shirts that never got really white, and suits that got stained at the cleaners, of maids that stole not only books but rifled drawers for socks and handkerchiefs, of rooms that never got warm enough, and martinis that never got cold enough, and bills unfairly rendered, of the landlord's endless complaints and self-delighting rages, the doctor's prescriptions that never worked, the waste of life itself to say nothing of fine economic theory. He coughed—by now a habit—and saw, as if it belonged to someone else, his hand at rest on the stone bannister, the fingers stained from smoking, the cuff faintly grey, distinctly frayed. He felt battered, and shabby and old and here was someone to block not only the flow of his grief, but the motion of his salvaging operation, that was to say, the direction of his return; for every step now was bringing him physically closer to the land he had had to come abroad to discover, the land where things rest on solid ground and reasons may be had upon request and business is conducted in the expected manner. It all meant more than he had ever suspected it did.

"Could you possibly tell me—you are an American, aren't you—I don't speak much Italian, none at all, in fact—maybe you even know who I'm looking for—does a Mrs. Ingram live here?"

"She isn't here just now, at least I don't think so. Come to think of it, she's out of the city, at least for the time being."

He grasped at remembering how she felt about it—about these people who kept coming. She did not like it; he knew that much. But a boy like this one, anybody on earth would want to see a boy like that. He retreated from her particular complexities, the subtly ramified turnings were a sharp renewal of pain, the whats and whys he could of course if necessary deal in had always been basically outside his character, foreign to him, in the way a clear effective answer was not foreign whether it was true or not.

"Very odd. I got her address just before leaving from the States."

"When was that?"

"Oh—ten days ago."

"Well then that explains it. She's only left a couple of weeks back, or so I understand."

He ran on down the stairs. The boy fell in step with him and they went out together. The fountain at the corner played with the simple delight of a child. "You see, I have this package, rather valuable, I think. I would have telephoned, but didn't know the language well enough—the idea scared me off. Now I've gone and rented this car to go to Naples in, that scares me too, but I guess I'll make it. I just wonder what to do with the package."

"Mail it—why not? Care of the consulate. She works there. Your hotel would do it, insured, everything."

"Did you know her well then? You see, I'm her nephew, by marriage, that is. When I was a boy, younger than now at least, she used to—"

"Listen, it's too bad you and I can't have a coffee or something, but I happen to be going to catch a plane."

They shook hands and parted. He had begun to feel that another moment's delay would have mired him there forever, that he had snatched back to himself in a desperate motion his very life. Walking rapidly, he turned a corner.

He went into a bar for coffee and was standing, leaning his elbow on the smooth surface and stirring when somebody said, "Hi, Jim!" and he looked up and there was Jean Coggins. She was eating a croissant and gave him a big grin, whiskery with crumbs. He laughed in some way he had not laughed for a year. "What d'you know?" he asked her. As usual, she didn't know anything back of yesterday. "I was going down to Capri yesterday but it rained. It even hailed! And that storm last night! Now look at it. Wouldn't it kill you?" "It shouldn't be allowed." He paid for her bill and his and while doing so wondered if at any time during the entire year in Italy she had ever actually paid for anything. She skimmed along beside him for a little way, going on like a little talking dog; he soon lost track of what she was saying; she always bored him—everything named Coggins bored him, but she was at least fresh and pretty. Walking, he flung an arm around her. "I heard from Alfredo," she said, "you remember in Venice?" "I remember something about some stamps," he said. She giggled.

(Because that day they got back from the Lido, with Martha out somewhere, or so the proprietor said, and the weather getting dim, the air covered with a closing sort of brightness, she had tried to buy stamps at the desk, feeling herself all salty in all the turns of her head and creases of her arms, but the proprietor said he was out of stamps and Jim Wilbourne going up the stairway, heard her, though it was already a flight up and half across the lobby, and he said, "I've got some stamps, so just stop by number something and I'll let you have them," but when she went and scratched at the door and thought he said Come in he was asleep—she must have known they weren't talking entirely about stamps, yet when he woke up scarcely knowing in the air's heaviness, the languor the surf had brought on and the boatride back, the lingering salt smell, exactly where he was, and saw her, he could not remember who she was, but said at once, "My God you've got the whitest teeth I ever saw," and pulled her down under his arm. But she didn't want to. She liked fighting, scuffling, maybe it was what she felt like, maybe it was because he was what she told him right out, an Older Man, which made him laugh though on the street that day coming out of the bar, almost exactly a year later, it wouldn't have been funny one bit, not one little bit; and then she had bitten him too, which was what he got for mentioning her teeth. Otherwise, she might not have thought about it. He had cuffed her. "Let's stay on," she said, "I love this place. All across Italy and couldn't even swim. That old lake was slimy. Anyway I'm in love with the boy at the desk. Get them to let us stay." "You mean get rid of your parents," he said, "that's what you're driving at. Or is it her too?" "You mean Martha? Well, she makes me feel dumb, but she's okay." She came up on one elbow, a sudden inspiration. "She likes you." "Oh, stop it." "I know." "How do you know?" "I just know. I always know. I can tell." "But maybe it's you that I—" "But it's Alfredo that I—" "Alfredo? Who's that?" "You don't ever listen. The boy at the desk." She had squirmed out from under and run off, snatching up a whole block of stamps off the table—he actually had had some stamps, though this surprised him, and later in the pensione walking around restless as a big animal in the lowering weather, he had heard her talking, chattering away to the boy who kept the desk, sure enough, right halfway down on the service stairs, and the little maids stepped over and around them with a smile: "Ti voglio bene, non ti amo; dimmi, dimmi—Ti voglio bene." One way to learn the language. He thumbed an ancient German magazine, restless in an alcove, and saw Martha Ingram go by; she had come in and quietly bathed and dressed, he supposed, her hair was gleaming, damp and freshly up, her scent floated in the darkening corridor, she did not see him, rounding the stairs unconsciously in the cloud of her own particular silence. Some guy had given her one hell of a time. He thought of following her, to talk, to what? He flipped the magazine aside; his thoughts roved, constricted in dark hallways. . . .)

"I've got his picture, want to see?" "I don't have time, honey." Next she would be getting his advice. She loved getting advice about herself. He told her goodbye, taking a sharp turn away. Would he ever see her again? The thought hardly brushed him.

(Would she ever see him again? The thought did not brush her at all. What did pass through her mind —erroneously, anyone but Jean Coggins would have thought [she did not know a word like that]—was a memory of one day she was in Rossi's, the fashion shop where she worked on the Via Boncompagni, and had just taken 10,000 lire from the till [and not for the first time], to lend to a ragazzo who took pictures on the Via Veneto and was always a little bit behind though he kept a nice seicento. She would have put it back before the lunch hour was over at four, but the signora found it gone and was about to fire her, though she denied having done it except as a loan to her mother's donna di servizio, who had forgotten money for the shopping and had passed by on the way to the market. She would bring it right back from home. She faded off toward the back of the shop, for the signora was waggling her head darkly, and working away in a undertone [Figurati!]. And while she was in the back, way back where the brocade curtains and satin wall-paper faded out completely and there were only the brown-wrapped packages of stuffs [tessuti] stacked up in corners of a bare room with a gas jet and a little espresso machine, and snips and threads strewn about the floor, she heard a voice outside and it was Martha Ingram and the signora was saying with great gentilezza, "O, signora, the American girl you sent me, the Signorina Co-gins . . ." and then she heard, in the level quiet poised educated voice, almost like a murmur: "Oh, no, there was some mistake about that. I never sent her to you, signora, there was some mistake. . . . However, nondimeno. . . . I am sure she is very good . . . È una brava ragazza, sono sicura. . . ." And then there was something about some gloves. Addio, she thought, in Italian. Adesso comincia la musica . . . now the music will really begin. She thought of running out the back door. She liked working up near the Veneto, where it was fun. And then the Signora Rossi herself appeared in her trim black dress with her nails all beautifully madreperla and her gold Florentine snake bracelet with the garnet eyes and her sleek jet hair scrolled to the side and her eyes that were always asked how many mila lire, and she twitched at the curtain and said, "Signorina Co-gins, you are a liar—it is always la stessa cosa. . . . You have given the money to that paparazzo, and the money was not even yours, but mine. It would have been gentile indeed if you had first asked me if *I*—io, io—had had some debt or other to pay. Davvero. But then I do not drive you out to Frascati in a seicento—not often, do I? No, not at all. But as for using the name of Signora Ingram, mia cliente, to come into mia casa di moda. . . ."

It went on and on like this, a ruffling stream of Italian, unending; as though she had stuck her head in a fountain, it went pouring past her ears. And then she remembered, out of her scolded-child exterior, that pensione in Venice, and Jim Wilbourne this time [rather than Alfredo]—the dim concept of the faceless three of them—him and her and Martha Ingram—afloat within those rain-darkening corridors and stairways. She remembered tumbling on the damp bed and how he was taller than she and that made her restless in some indefinable way, so she said what was true: "She likes you." "Oh, stop it." "I know." "How do you know?" "I just know, I always know, I can tell." For the truth was she was not at all a liar: she was far more honest than anybody she knew. It was the signora who had said all along, just because she said she knew Martha Ingram, that she had been sent there by Martha Ingram who was close to the ambassador, and the signora could tell more lies while selling a new gown than Jean Coggins had ever told in her life, and another truth she knew was that Martha Ingram was bound to come in and "tell on her" someday to the signora. It had been a certainty, a hateful certainty, because women like Martha would always fasten to one man at a time. She remembered her awe of Martha Ingram, her even wishing in some minor way to be like her. And then she saw it all, in a flash; perhaps, like that, she turned all the way into her own grown-up self, and would never want to be like anybody else again, for she suddenly pushed out of the corner where a tatter of frayed curtain concealed a dreary little delivery entrance from even being glimpsed by accident by anyone in the elegant negozio, started up and flung herself full height, baring her teeth like a fox, and spit out at the signora: "Che vuole? Non sono una donna di servizio. I am not a servant. Faccio come voglio . . . I will do as I like. Faccio come mi pare . . . I will do as I please. Che vuole?"

There was a sudden silence, rather like somebody had died, and the street door to the negozio could be heard to open. Signora Rossi broke into a laugh, at first an honest laugh—possibly the only one she had ever given

—shading immediately into a ripple of pleasant amusement of the elegant padrona at her pretty little assistente; she turned on her narrow black stiletto heels and having touched her hair, folded her hands in that certain pleasing way, and moved toward the door.)

When Jim Wilbourne reached his own apartment, there at the head of the first flight of steps which ran down into the open courtyard, the landlord was lurking, paunchy and greasy-haired with a long straight nose and tiny whistle-sized mouth, a walking theatre of everything that had been done to him by the Wilbournes and all he could do in return because of it; here was the demon, the one soul who proved that inferno did exist, at least in Italy. Jim Wilbourne felt the back of his neck actually stiffen at the sight of Signor Micozzi in his white linen suit. The demon's energy, like the devastating continuous inexhaustible energy of Italy, was always fresh and ready for the fray; the time was always now. "Jesus, another round," Jim Wilbourne thought; "will I die before I leave this place?" Smoking, saying nothing, he climbed the stair to within two steps of the waiting figure which had bought that new white suit, it would seem, especially to quarrel in. The two of them, on perfect eye level, stared at one another. Jim Wilbourne dropped his cigarette, stepped on it, and walked deliberately past. His hand was on the bolt when the first words fell in all the smear of their mock courtesy:

"Scusi un momento, Signor Wilbourne, per cortesia."

For a moment, at the door, they ran through the paces of their usual nasty exchange. It was all he could do to keep from striking physically; in Italy that would have involved him so deeply he would never be free; Italy was the original tar baby; he knew that; getting out was the thing now; he had a sense of salvage and rescue, of swimming the ocean.

"Scusi, scusi!"

"Prego!"

They were shouting by now, their mutual contempt oozing wretchedly out of every word. He stepped inside and slammed the door.

His wife poked her head into the corridor. She was working; she was always working. Thin, in a pair of knee-length slacks of the sort nobody at all in Italy wore, which hung awkwardly, showing how much weight she'd lost in one nagging illness after another, her dark hair lank and flat, lying close to her head, framing like two heavy pencil lines her sharp face and great flat eyes: "All that bastard had to do was stand a few inches to the left when he passed the window, and I would have dropped this right on him," she said. She pointed to a ceramic umbrella stand she had made herself. It must have weighed seventy pounds at least. Her voice, slightly hoarse by nature with a ready tough fundamental coarseness in everything she observed when they were alone (she was never much "like herself" with other people), was a sort of life to him. He could not even remember life without it. "They called from the university about some survey on Neapolitan family management. It was due last week. I called your office but nobody answered." "I was there all morning but nobody rang." A world of old quarrels hung in shadowy phalanxes between every word of an exchange like this one, but both of them wearied to pour enough energy into any one of them to make it live. He stood in the doorway of her studio where she had even hung up a Van Gogh reproduction—the whole place looked American now. The Italian furniture had acquired the aspect of having been bought in a Third Avenue junk shop. "The dear old telephone system," she said, turning away, the corner of her mouth bitten in. He picked up the paper and stood reading it, leaning against a gilded chest of drawers, pushing at the dark hair above his ear with restless fingers. How would she have picked it up, he wondered, the umbrella stand? She would doubtless have managed. It was then the phone started ringing. "If that's the landlord—" he said. He knew it was. It was a favorite trick of Signor Micozzi, when the door slammed in his face, to circle down to the bar on the corner and ring upstairs, continuing the argument without the loss of a syllable. Martha Ingram would never get into this sort of mess— The thought wrote itself off the page. He crashed the paper to the floor. His wife whirled around and saw the way he looked. "Now, Jim, please—!"

"Look, you realize how much deposit he took on this place? Three hundred and fifty dollars. If he so much as hesitates about giving it back." "That's what he came for! Of course, he hesitates. He's never had the slightest intention of giving it back." "All right. Okay. He's in for a surprise or two." "But not to him, not to him! Don't you touch him!" She suddenly began to sob without crying, a grating desperate sound, biting out between the jerks of her breath, "If you touch him we'll never get out of here, we'll be here forever in this country, this horrible place, I'll die, I'll die here!" She leaped at him, latching onto his arm with both hands, and she had grown so light and he had grown so angry that when he lifted his arm she came up with it, right off the floor, as handy as a monkey. They both began to laugh—it was ludicrous, and it must have been soon after that they started figuring things out.

Her cry was over; she had even combed her hair.

Then she began to bully and mock and dare him slightly; as totally disenchanted as ever, she had begun to be herself again. In some ways he listened, in others he didn't have to; most of all he was drawn back to where he was a few streets after he departed from Jean Coggins for all eternity, when, abruptly halting in a little crooked alley all alone, at some equidistance—mentally speaking, at least—between Martha and his wife, he gave over to wonder; for the first time, astringent and hard with himself, he allowed it to happen, he allowed the wonder to operate; fully, beautifully, he watched it curve and break in a clean magnificent wave.

What had he taken there, what had he conquered, so much as a city—a white, ample, ripe city, with towers, streets, parks, treasures? One bold leap of the imagination back there in Venice (the sort of thing he had always wanted to do but had never brought off quite so perfectly) had taken him soaring across the stale and turgid moat of her surrounding experience, had landed him at her very gates. It had been all blindly impulsive, perhaps cruel; but one thing had to be said for it—it had worked.

But there was something he knew and this was it: he could never have created her, and a thousand times, in turning her head, or putting on a glove, she had silently, unconsciously, praised whoever had put her together, ironically, the object of their merciless destruction—Jesus, what a trap! He rebelled at the whole godawful picture: it wasn't true. Love did not have to refer to anybody; that could all be changed in five minutes of wanting to. He had only to tell her, say so, absolutely— For an instant his mind crazed over like shattered glass, and it was some time before he hauled himself together, as though after another blind charge, this time at a wall, the first of many. Was it there or later, he allowed himself—briefly, but he did allow it—a moment's wonder at himself recognizing a young man not even thirty and what he had challenged, taken, known. He knew in what sense he was the possessor still, and in what sense no matter when he left he would always be.

(About here he came to a corner, and frowning, leaned against a wall. Grace Hartwell saw him; she was coming down from the dressmaker, hurrying home to pack.)

He was clearly aware of the many ways in which his Italian year wore the aspect of failure, of an advance halted, his professional best like chariot wheels miring in the mud, nothing, in short, to be proud of.

He walked on, at last, with a dogged, almost classical, stubbornness. This was what it had worn down to. He would live beyond himself again; he would, in future, be again gleaming and new, set right like a fine mechanism; he had to go to the States for that. But in this hour, blazed at by a sudden foreign sun, he presented to himself neither mystery nor brilliance, any more than he did to his wife or the landlord, in whose terms he did not even despise to live, if only his energy held out till the shores of Italy dropped behind him forever. But Martha too had been Italy—a city, his own, sinking forever. There was the wall again, blank and mocking. He could go crashing into it again, over and over and over, as many times as he wanted to.

15

It was George Hartwell who got the full force of the Wilbourne departure after they had left Rome earlier than they had said they were going to, in the night. Now every day or so, the landlord, Signor Micozzi, called Hartwell and "Yes," he said, "Va bene," he said, and "Grazie, signor console, molto gentile, sissignore," said Signor Micozzi.

Hartwell gave Signor Micozzi appointments when no one else could get one, while the important people went across the hall to see Martha; he swivelled back in his chair and listened and listened . . . his mind wandered, sometimes he dozed, he could pick up the refrain whenever he cared to. "Gente cattiva, quei Wilbourne. Cosa potevo fare . . . cosa? Sono assolutaménte senza . . ."

"Ma Signor Micozzi, lei ha già ricevuto il deposito, non è vero?"

"Si, ma questo, signor console, non deve pensare che il deposito è abbastanza per questo . . . hanno rottoo tutto! . . . Tutto è rovinato!"

One day soon now, he was going to haul himself together. One has to wake oneself; one cannot go on forever, unravelling the waste, the inconsequential portions of a dream that was not even one's own. So one day soon now he was going to stop it. He was going to say, like any tourist in the market, Quanto allora? He might even write a check. It was his American conscience, that was it. . . .

Poor George Hartwell, there was one success he had had. Everyone assured him of it—the Coggins', of course. He could take pride in them; who would have thought that Italians would let any American tell them about opera?

He left Martha's doorway. The sun struck him a glorious blow and the little fountain pulsed from white to green in the new season.

Ah, yes, the Coggins'. Veni, vidi, vici.

He looked for his car and found it. Dorothy, Richard, and Jean.

They had gone off triumphantly to take the boat at Genoa, had been waved off at the station by contingents of Roman friends, leaving time to go by Venice and revisit that same pensione, having sent on ahead to the boat crate upon crate of tourist junk, a whole case of country wines (a gift from the landlord, by now a lifelong friend). There were also a package of citations and awards from a dozen appreciative music companies, autographed photos of half the singers in Italy, and ninety percent of all the chocolate in Perugia which had been showered upon Jean by admirers from Trastavere to the Parioli, from Milan to Palermo. Perhaps at this moment, she was talking to Alfredo again in the pensione, giggling at his soft Venetian accent, all in a palazzo set on waters crackling in the brilliant light, or strolling about the garden, hearing a motorboat churn past. Waiting for Sunday dinner in the central hallways, with one or two of the same old guests and the proprietor with his head in the books . . . waiting for Sunday dinner. It was a Western tradition, a binding point for the whole world. And why not? In his vision of Venice, for a moment, Martha Ingram and all her long mad vision stood redeemed. But not for long. Jim Wilbourne was never far enough away; his head turned slowly, his regard scorched slowly across the scene; as though the Coggins' had been in an eighteenth-century engraving deployed in each pleasant detail about their Venetian casa, the edges curled, the loosely woven paper bent backward, the images distorted, changed—one turned away.

Hartwell at last got home and opened windows in an empty flat, fetched bread and cheese from the kitchen, fought steadily against the need for whiskey, and sat down to unlock the dispatch case. His wife, so easily evoked, crossed the ocean at his nod to stand at his elbow and remark with her warm wit that along with all those dispatches, briefings, summaries, minutes, and memoranda from the embassy, he might possibly draw out a poison toad, a severed hand, some small memento of Martha Ingram.

But he did not.

The reports she had done for him were smooth and crisp, brilliant, unblemished. Their cutting edge was razor-keen, their substance unrolled like bolts of silk. There was nothing to add, nothing to take away. It was sinister, and he did not want to think about it alone. But he had to. Who has been destroyed in this as much as me? he wondered. Gordon Ingram is not alone. No, it was against George Hartwell's present and fond breast that the hurled spear struck.

Knowing this, he could not stand it any longer.

Getting up, slamming out, he got into his car and went

nosing about the streets again. The Grand Hotel, a Sunday vision also, elegance and the Grand Tour, too little exercise, every wish granted, marmalade for tea, and if you're willing to pay extra, tours can be arranged through the— He had charged halfway across the lobby before he stopped to think, to enquire.

"A little signora americana in blue, sissignore. She is there, eccola là."

And there she was. He saw her. She was real. Martha was not that crazy.

She was over in a far corner before some enormous windows reaching to the ceiling, canopied with drawn satin portieres, and she was not alone. The Italian floorcleaner who had mopped and dusted the lobby there for at least ten years but had never once before this moment sat down in one of the sofas was now beside her. She had gone upstairs, and using her dictionary (as Hartwell was later to hear) had written down the message which she had to give to someone, and now she was reading it off. A piece of light blue letter paper trembled in her little crooked hand.

"Ho un amico che sta morendo . . . I have a friend who is dying. Questa mattina ho ricevuto la notizia . . . only this morning I received the news."

"O signora!" cried the floorcleaner. "Mi dispiace . . . I am so sorry!" He leaned toward her; his small-featured Latin face wrung instantly with pity; he also had lost friends.

"Mio amico era sempre buono . . . è buono . . . buono. . . ."

It was then that George Hartwell appeared. The floorcleaner sprang to his feet. "S'accomodi . . . sit down," said Hartwell. "In nome di Dio."

There was no one really around. The bright day was subdued to the décor of the great outdated windows, which made a humble group of them. And really, thought Hartwell, I've got no business here, what am I doing with these two people? Once I had a little kingdom here. It is stolen, it is gone. Should I tell them? Would they cry?

He sat and listened.

Now the sentiment, the inaccuracy, of the usual human statement was among them; irresistibly as weeds in a great ruin, it was springing up everywhere around what was being said of Gordon Ingram. His books, his wisdom, his circle of friends, his great heart, his sad life. . . . Hartwell was translating everything to the floorcleaner, who had forgotten that he was a floorcleaner. He was, above all, a human being, and he accordingly began to weep.

George Hartwell told the lady in blue that Martha Ingram was out of town.

6

On a day that now seemed long, long ago, had seemed long ago, in fact, almost the precipitate instant its final event occurred, she had gone out of her apartment which Jim Wilbourne had been in for an hour or so, for the last time. It was a matter of consideration to them both to give him time to get well away before she went out behind him, leaving rooms she could not for the moment bear to be alone in. She did not know that he had been delayed on the stair. She saw him, however, come out of the bar with Jean Coggins, laughing with her over something; she stepped back, almost from the curb into the street which at that point was narrow, damp, still in winter shadow; and then a car passed and she looked up in time to see

Gordon Ingram's nephew driving by. She never doubted that was who it was. He had grown a lot, that was all. He did not see her; the car nosed into a turning which led away from her, away, she realized too late, icily, from her apartment. He had been there already; he had gone. From out of sight, in the chilly labyrinth where the sun would slowly seep in now and warm and dry and mellow through the long summer months, she heard Jean Coggins laugh. The boy had grown so much; she used to give him books and read to him: what college was he in, would no one tell her? She had stopped still—after her first futile steps, begun too late, of running after the car—in a small empty square. The direction of the car pulled against the direction of the laugh, in an exact mathematical pivot, herself being the central point of strain, and in this counterweight, she felt her life tear almost audibly, like ripping silk. She leaned against a wall and looked out on the little empty space, an opening in the city. The sun brought out the smell of cigarettes, but no one was about; only dumb high doorways and shadows sliced at a clear, straight angle across a field of sun.

He was driven away from me, she thought: Jim Wilbourne did it; I know that it is true. I am no more than that meeting point of shadow and sun. It is everything there is I need to know, that I am that and that is me.

It was the complex of herself that her spirit in one motion abandoned; those intricate structures, having come to their own completion, were no longer habitable. She saw them crumble, sink and go under forever. And here was what was left: a line of dark across a field of sun.

When the small package arrived for Martha—a strand of pearls which had belonged to an aunt who had left them to her in memory of—she hardly read the letter, which was not from Gordon Ingram but from the nephew who was now in Greece. The lettering on the package had been done by Gordon Ingram. There was no message inside. She went carefully, in a gentle way, downstairs and laid the strand in the crevice of the palazzo wall, like an offering to life. She felt as a spirit might, rather clever, at being able to move an object or leave a footprint. Some Italian would be telling the story for many years, waving the pearls aloft. "Dal cielo! Dal cielo! Son cadute dal cielo!"

George Hartwell's saying to the lady in blue that Martha was out of town was no lie; perhaps he was incapable of telling one. She was driving to the sea to meet Roberto there, possibly the sister and the sister's husband, possibly not, the plans were generous, promising, and vague. She more and more arranged to do things alone, a curious tendency, for loneliness once had been a torment, whereas now she regarded almost everything her eyes fell on with an equal sense of companionship; her compatibility was with the world. The equality of it all could of course be in some purely intellectual, non-nervous way disturbing. Things were not really equal, nor were people; one explanation might be that she simply did not care very deeply about anything, the emotional target she had once plainly furnished had disappeared. Was this another name for freedom? Freedom was certainly what it felt like. She bent with complete compassion, fleshless, invisible and absent, above the rapidly vanishing mortality of Gordon Ingram, at the same time she swung happily, even giddily (there went that streak again, the necessary madness), around the Colosseum, where the fresh glittering traffic, like a flight of gulls, joyous in the sunlight, seemed to float and lilt, fearless of collision. Children's bones and women's skulls had been dug up there and conjectures could be easily formed about what sort of undemocratic accidents had overtaken these fine people, but now the old ruin stood noble and ornamental to

Rome, and views of it were precious to those apartments which overlooked it.

Faceless and nameless, the throng rushed on; they always had and would forever, as long as the city stood.

It was not Gordon Ingram who had died, nor was it Jim Wilbourne who was absent. It was herself, she thought. I am gone, she thought; they have taken me with them; I shall never return.

If only George Hartwell could understand that, he would know better about things, he could even bear them. But then, she saw, he might be compelled to trace a similar path in his own life; for knowing it arose merely, perhaps only, from being it. Let him be spared, she thought; let him be his poor human soul forever.

She was of those whom life had held a captive and in freeing herself she had met dissolution, and was a friend now to any landscape, a companion to cloud and sky.

Elizabeth Spencer is acknowledged as one of America's outstanding writers of fiction. Her most recent novel, the best-selling *The Light in the Piazza*, made her the recipient of the McGraw-Hill Fiction Award for 1960. Her first novel, *Fire in the Morning*, appeared in 1948 and was declared one of the three best first novels of that year. The second, *This Crooked Way*, was published in 1952 and the next year she received a Guggenheim Fellowship which took her to Italy. *The Voice at the Back Door* (McGraw-Hill, 1956), her third novel, won several literary awards and was a commercial as well as critical success. Miss Spencer is married to John Rusher of Cornwall, England, and they now make their home near Montreal.